I0558920

The Rot is Deep
An O Line Mystery

M. Saylor Billings

Billibatt Productions

The Rot is Deep - An O Line Mystery

Library of Congress Catalog Card Number: 2012908310

ISBN: 0983806152
ISBN 13: 978-0-9838061-5-8
Billibatt Productions
www.billibatt.com
www.olinemysteries.com
olinemysteries@gmail.com

For Claude LaFayette

In Memoriam

M. Saylor Billings

TABLE OF CONTENTS

Coming Soon from M. Saylor Billings

Red, White, and Scotch: Book 4 of
The O Line Mysteries Series

The O Line Mystery Short Stories

Writing as Lorna Tollison:
Nobody, really, Likes You
A Guide to Insouciance.

PROLOGUE

Code named "Aurora Shield," the satellite cloaking device tricks any satellite tracking networks into believing they are tracking space rocks or space detritus. By using magnets and mirrors in the housing and coding the software to replicate the radio signals that would bounce off space detritus back to earth, the cloaking device makes the satellite and its functions virtually invisible. The brilliant simplicity of Aurora's design shares the same survival functions animals have developed through evolution. It should have been code named "Chameleon."

Several reconnaissance and space surveillance agencies had been working on their own 'invisibility shields' and jamming devices for years. But it was a small geospatial software company, The Hayward, located in the sprawling Northern California coastal town of Hayward, that perfected the cloaking trick of the satellite trade and sold their idea to No Such Agency, the NSA.

Originally, The Hayward had been contracted to create mapping software for Spectorgies' defense contracting sector, whose main customers are the sixteen members of the national intelligence agencies. It was through Spectorgies' employees that the NSA had gotten wind of The Hayward's cloaking device. The NSA, however, skipped the Spectorgies' middlemen and contracted The Hayward directly. With the increasing threat of a cyber attacks from both in and out of the country, it was imperative that the building and launching of such a powerful surveillance unit remain an 'Eyes Only' project. In an effort to keep their new satellite asset a secret for as long as possible, the NSA used The Hayward's hardware design and paid EarthSat, a satellite maker in San Diego, for the hardware construction.

Tim steered his car into the parking space marked: VISITOR. The nondescript cement building among a street of identical nondescript cement buildings looked more like a distribution administration building for car parts or toilet tissue than a high-tech software company. He smiled at Sergey His-last-name-has-no-vowels strolling languidly over to his car. He met Sergey yesterday during the initial human resource meeting he conducted here at The Hayward and realized that it may be too late for these employees to emerge into a working group. Tim considered Sergey to be a typical software coder, unbelievably bright, but completely without social skills. But the rest of the software engineers social skills had morphed into a scene played out in *Lord of the Flies*.

"I have family in Ukraine and I tell them I work at *The* Hayward *in* Hayward, California. They think we own the town." Sergey pointed to the visitor's sign in front of Tim's car and said, "Why don't you park in back, behind the fence, since you will be here all day. I'll have them open the gates for you."

As Sergey went inside Tim started his car and pulled out again. He waited in front of the gate and flipped through a file folder, Sergey Smrz, and turned the page to a handwritten note. Smurtz. "Smurtz." He practiced it a couple of times as the gate slid back. Considering his own last name, Doughall, is pronounced "Doyle," Tim felt a kinship to the young Ukrainian. And it was important for a human resource specialist be able to pronounce everyone's name, with or without vowels.

At the sudden shrill of his cell phone, Tim gripped the steering wheel tighter and inhaled sharply. Finally, as he parked the car again, he slowly let out his breath. Glancing in the rearview mirror and giving his short brown hair a pat, he gave himself a relaxed, reassuring smile. He clicked the cell phone silent and nodded earnestly in the mirror.

Tim's life had been snowballing out of control for the past year or more. Tim could trace the beginning of the snowball's path to his former employer being bought by the conglomerate Spectorgies, whose reach involved everything from defense contracts, software development, bio-tech companies, weapons development, to, oddly, infant wear. That's when Tim had been tapped as an informant to the NSA. Spectorgies had overseas companies and contracts with foreign governments; so, at that time, Tim believed it to be his civic duty to inform on them if necessary. Then the FBI contacted him to inform on the NSA's relationship with Spectorgies. But when his handler at the FBI was murdered, he decided his first allegiance must be to himself and his wife, Annie. He looked down at the cell phone. The display read: Annie. She must have gotten the divorce papers, he thought.

Tim followed the sidewalk around the corner and entered the building. Placing his two bags on the screener belt and emptying his pockets, he walked though the metal detector. Yesterday, Tim had not met this particular elderly security guard who wore a wig under his cap and two sets of glasses hanging from ropes across his potbelly. He tried not to stare at the older man as he limped over to his clipboard.

"Mr. Doug-Hall?" The security guard asked, smiling up from his clipboard.

"Yes."

"You're to go to the boardroom, down the hall on the left."

"What is that anyway?" The guard asked as glanced at the security monitor.

"It's my projector. It makes doing presentations easier if I have a lot of information to go over." Tim pulled out a box of donuts and offered one to the guard, but the elderly guard declined the offer, patting his potbelly.

"What'll they think of next?" The security guard turned the conveyor belt back on and handed Tim his bag and said wearily, "Bathrooms are down the hall and around the corner."

"Thanks." Tim flashed his confident smile and walked down the hall.

Tim busied himself setting out the donuts and boxes of coffee in the boardroom. His handler with the FBI, Michael, had been adamant in his instructions. Tim understood his role here was at the dangerous, small end of the whip. Officially, this day was to be the end of a long and tenuous FBI investigation into The Hayward's contracts with Spectorgies through the NSA. Unofficially, he knew there was more to it than that. And he was to report to the NSA, to the best of his knowledge, the full extent of the relationship between Spectorgies and The Hayward. He just needed to get through this day and he was done. He had been working the equivalent of three jobs for the past year: his regular job, but also his gig as an informant to the NSA about his regular job and also as an informant to the FBI. And they all paid. It wasn't enough to retire on, but enough to get as much distance between Annie and himself as possible for a while, until the smoke cleared.

Sergey walked into the boardroom as Tim finished setting up his laptop and projector.

"You're like the pied piper with donuts, Tim. Yes, you get more with honey and vinegar."

"Yes, but it's *than* vinegar. More with honey *than* with vinegar."

"I like vinegar. Every morning teaspoon, my grandmother taught me."

"Some things are universal, aren't they?"

"Tim, do you know any nice girl I could marry?"

Tim paused and thought. "I don't know. Let me think." He poured himself a cup of coffee and grinned. "I think all the nice girls are married. I know some nice guys?"

Sergey was bewildered. "Tim! You are turd burglar?"

Tim hadn't heard that phrase since the eighth grade. "No. Sergey. The phrase is gay or homosexual. We don't say that or fudge-packer or anything derogatory involving sexual acts. Which is exactly why I'm here with you guys today. Could you round up the other people who are attending the seminar?"

"We'll break for lunch about noon and reconvene at one? How does that sound?" Tim looked around the room of a dozen or so goggle-eyed faces and resumed. "So, okay, yesterday, we were working on the employment packets in sections, so after lunch, I'll just open it up to individual questions you may have. You guys can come and go and we'll do the questions one on one. Oh, and I wanted to thank Sergey for his hospitality. After I go, if you guys have any questions about the human resources packet or anything please don't hesitate to give me a call."

More stares.

"You're welcome, Tim. Thank you for spending the time with us." Sergey beamed at him.

Tim tapped his laptop alive and clicked on the projector but nothing happened. He flicked the on switch and tinkered with the cord as everyone waited.

"I'm sorry, just give me a minute here," Tim said looking around. This is it, the moment he'd planned for all week. But whoever was his FBI counterpart was not jumping in. Maybe not yet, he thought, and continued fiddling around with the projector. "Guys, um, I'm sorry, I was going to go over some slides here but it looks like my projector has had it, I'm afraid. But I do have a plan B. I don't think I brought enough copies but we could share some of these worksheets and go over it that way."

"Don't we have one of those?" Someone from the group spoke up, indicating the projector.

"Yes, but it's in Mr. Hodge's office," Sergey replied.

"And there are two in the supply cabinet," someone else said.

A young man got up. "I'll get it for ya'," and left the room.

Tim smiled. "Well, I guess this is like having a heart attack in a hospital." He picked up his own projector and moved it to the back of the room and set it on a chair next to the door so his counterpart could make the switch. He felt his muscles go weak for a moment as the relief shot through him. Calm and casual, he thought.

"Where's Hodge?" he heard a man mutter.

"I think he's in uh, San Diego," another responded.

"And by that you mean, Vegas."

"No, man, he's in Phoenix. He's got a thing down there."

"What thing?" someone asked. "Is it on two legs?"

The young man came back in with a projector and helped Tim set it up. The chatter stopped and Tim continued his presentation by rote.

According to Michael, the entire device was supposed to be put together here and sold to the NSA. Unless the NSA had already got wind of this second mock up, being made here at The Hayward. What if the NSA knew about his informing for the FBI? Maybe he was just a pawn between the two agencies. It's not possible that the NSA got Spectorgies to make some kind of deal with The Hayward to get Tim in here for a human resource session, because that would reveal him as a NSA informant. Tim's mind swam through the dark sea of possibilities of what could happen to him when he walked out of here with a multi-multi-million dollar piece of technology. Would it ever be possible to be safe after this day?

A momentary glance from Sergey brought him back. "Sergey, a question?"

Sergey got up and walked to the back of the room. "Yeah, which one of you ate the last cruller?"

"Okay, moving on…" Tim started again moving through the slides again while reciting his speech. Another part of his mind was already moving on through the rest of the day. He was to meet Michael at their usual safe house, a room above the Lemon Suds bar on Ohlone Island. They hadn't met there in a while and Tim hoped Michael had gotten the bathroom working again as he would need to stay there for a few days before heading back to Spectorgies home office in Phoenix and making his report to the NSA.

CHAPTER 1

MOVING IN, AGAIN

As Lorna Tollison placed the final book on her new bookshelves in the front room of her craftsman bungalow, the phone rang. "Hello."

"My flight's leaving in about an hour. Are you still okay to pick me up?" Sally asked.

"What? You're not supposed to come home until tomorrow."

Sally Thompson looked around the Phoenix airport and measured her next words. Her partner, Lorna, had been dealing with a lot of change recently with the move into their first home and Lorna's father's insistence on visiting so he could help fix the place up. But also Lorna had closed up her web content publishing business and finished her first satirical novel, to very little fan-fare. On top of all that, Sally had left town for a week when her own Grandmother had a stroke and had asked Sally to help her move into an elderly care facility. "I'm sorry," Sally said. "If I told you wrong, can I come home now?"

"Yes. What time do you land?"

"One-thirty."

"I'll meet you at the baggage claim. I have so much to tell you. Wait until you see the house."

"Uh oh."

"Uh oh nothing. It's beautiful!" Lorna said, patting the new bookshelf.

"What did he do?"

"Well, basically we have a whole new kitchen, just – you'll see. I don't want to ruin the surprise."

"That makes me feel a little guilty."

"Not compared to how guilty you're going to feel when you see it."

"Really?"

"Yep. And I've got more news."

"I just talked to you last night!" Sally exclaimed.

"Tim's going through with the divorce from Annie."

"Shut. Up."

"I know. You absorb *that* and we'll dissect the events when you get home."

"Okay. So, Tessa next?"

"Yes, Tessa arrives the day after tomorrow. I think." Lorna looked down at her desk calendar. "Yep. Today's the 9th."

"It's the 10th," Sally muttered softly.

"How did I lose a day?"

"Well, let's see…for the past two months your life has been turned sideways. And then I leave town for a week, leaving you to finish the remodeling with your dad, plus your sister's coming to visit. Give yourself a break."

"You haven't talked to Tessa have you?" Lorna asked.

"No. I've had my hands full too."

"She's being kinda cagey. She says it's just a visit and then my dad let it slip that she has business."

"Does it matter?"

"No. I just don't like the weirdness. Okay, see you in a little while."

"I love you."

"I love you too."

Lorna hung up and walked back into the living room. Their two large yellow tabbies, Patience and Fortitude, were passed out on the couch. Lorna looked around and frowned. There was something wrong. The feng shui was off or maybe it was the lack of furniture or what they had didn't match together. Maybe they needed a decorator.

"This room is annoying me," Lorna said to the cats.

Patience popped his head up and yawned at her.

Lorna walked through the archway door into the kitchen where the sun streamed in above the sink and counters. She liked everything about this room: the butter yellow walls, the glassed in cupboards, and the new appliances. This room is good, she thought. It feels like home.

Moving down the hall past the empty formal dining room and half bath, she poked her head into her office. Her father had built a catwalk with little stairs around the walls, starting where he had built little cat window beds. It was her dream office. It had a cramped sense of movement and urgency about it, a holdover feeling she enjoyed from working in New York City. Lorna took the stairs up to the bedrooms when a thought hit her. Did Sally know about Tim already? Sally and Tim are pretty good friends. Had Tim already told her about his plan? No, Sally can't keep a secret from her, especially one that would directly affect their relationship with her best friend Annie. Lorna brushed the idea out of her mind and turned on the shower.

The drive to the Oakland airport from Ohlone Island takes fifteen minutes, in heavy traffic. Most drivers take the highways so driving by way of Ohlone's back streets and across the estuary West Bridge are a straight shot. Lorna made it in ten minutes and waited at the baggage carousel. Lorna's chest rose in excitement as she caught sight of Sally at the top of the escalator. She had been so occupied over the last month with the book and so busy with her father over the last week that she hadn't really realized how very much she had missed her partner. Sally barely made it off the escalator when Lorna embraced her. "You're a sight for sore eyes."

"I missed you too. I'm glad to be home."

"So, how was your grandma?"

"Forget Grandma. How's Annie?" Sally replied.

Lorna regretted her question immediately. She pulled away and they sauntered over to the carousel. She knew that Sally always deflected any attempt to discuss her family. It was a touchy subject that Lorna tried to steer clear of. Her grandmother in Connecticut raised Sally while her parents worked in various embassies around the globe. Then her parents died in a car crash after Sally graduated college. It was a common past for both of them - Lorna had lost her mother when she was twelve, but, unlike Sally, Lorna had her father and Tessa, her adopted older sister, who helped fill in some of the gap. She gave Sally a pitying smile. "Are you okay?"

"Yeah. Oh, no. I'm good. The stroke was really minor I think, and the place she's moving to is a palace. She's got her own apartment in a high rise, 24-hour medical facility, two pools, a recreation area, cafeteria, and it's next to a golf course. They have a bus that runs four times a day in and out of the shopping mall and every other weekend goes to the casinos. No, Gram is doing just fine. We should all be so lucky."

"I'm so glad then." Lorna changed the subject quickly and dug in her bag. "Oh here, I thought you'd want some water," she said, handing Sally a bottle of water. "Dad made chicken soup or we can stop for something on the way if you want."

"Quill's chicken soup, please," Sally smiled. "And a side of gossip."

The carousel started up. As they took positions next to the rotating belt Lorna said, "Did you know about Tim's feelings? I mean, did you know about the divorce? Does he have some hoochie on the side?"

"Tim? Tim Doughall? No. Lorna, I'm just as shocked as everyone else. Tim has a hoochie? That's so unlike him."

"I don't know if he does or not but ya' know, he had to tell someone about this and I just thought since you guys hung out…"

"No. Anyway I would have told you first."

Lorna nodded, looking around. "Which is why he wouldn't tell you."

"Do you really think -- Tim? I could never see him cheating on Annie. It would be like watching a fish walk."

Lorna smiled at Sally and nodded. "Good one." Before Lorna and Sally met in New York City, Lorna had worked very hard on losing her Atlanta drawl. Too many times she had been laughed at and cruelly mimicked by complete strangers when she spoke. But she never lost the quips and sayings that someone raised in the South often ascribes to given situations. Sally had learned, for example, how far down the road "a piece" was and how much *more* sugar should be contained in "a pinch." She was completely charmed by the unique culture Lorna had grown up in, and she now often said she was "fixin'" to do something or she was "shittin' in tall cotton" or, like now, she would come up with her own quips.

Once they got home Lorna stopped Sally at the front door. "I feel like you should close your eyes."

"Why?"

"I don't know. Because it's exciting, I guess. But look, if you don't like anything, we can change it."

"I'm sure it's fine. Come on, open the door." Sally gave a little bounce of anticipation.

Patience and Fortitude situated themselves around the front door to greet them as Lorna pulled in Sally's suitcase. Sally picked up Fortitude and squeezed him as Patience stretched up on his hind legs for a pet as well. She handed Fortitude over to Lorna and picked up Patience giving him several head butts in return. The two cats busied themselves with the suitcase inspection as Sally began to walk around admiring the detail work Quill had put into their home.

"Wait till you see my office," Lorna said.

Sally was speechless as she walked into the kitchen, but finally found words. "Ohhhh. I mean, wow. He did this in a week?"

"We worked from dawn till dusk, every day. Come see my office. He did it all himself."

They made their way down the hall to Lorna's office. Sally gave an uncharacteristic squeal. "Ah! I love it. I want to be a cat." Sally got a close inspection of the cat stairway on the wall. "How did he do this without putting a million holes in the walls? Look at this bookcase Lorna! It's beautiful!"

"I know!"

"Where's my phone?" Sally patted her pockets.

"I don't know. Why?"

"I have to call your dad. I can't believe this!"

"You haven't seen the rest of the house."

"I don't care."

Sally made her way to the front door and picked through her bag, snapping up her cell phone and dialing.

"I'll heat up the soup," Lorna said, passing by on her way into the kitchen.

"Hi Quill. I'm speechless...No, it's just, I just can't absorb it – it's all so well done...I haven't even been upstairs...the kitchen and Lorna's office. Well, thank you from the bottom of my pea-packin' heart."

A crash from the kitchen made Sally swivel her head around to see Lorna, hanging on to the counter with her head dropped down, shaking her shoulders.

"Picking...Pea pickin' heart...well, I don't think I could ever express...I love you too.... yeah. She's doing great she moved into this – it's kinda a halfway home for the elderly, but very exclusive, pools, casino trips, 24-hour medical staff, she wears one of those life alerts. She's doing better now than before her stroke...okay, well thanks again. Bye."

Quill had walked into Tessa's converted barn, which now held her office, lab and the apartment for her assistant, Perez. He carefully folded his long frame down in his usual chair, across from her desk and looked at the print portrait of Leonhard Euler, the blind mathematician, which hung on the wall behind her.

"Where's Perez?" he asked.

Tessa brushed back her wild mane of curly red hair and shut down some of her electronics gadgetry on the desk. "He ran out to do a little shopping for us."

Quill hung his head. "Tell me again why I'm spying on my daughter like a Peeping Tom?"

"First of all, we're monitoring. Not spying. Secondly, it's not for Lorna. It's for me. I'll shut it down after I turn over the prototype and before I leave. It's just a precaution. I need to make sure no one is—"

"Then stay in a hotel or send Perez," Quill said, his voice rising and reflecting how tired he was and how nervous he was getting about their contract with this particular defense contractor.

In the world of geek, Tessa is a rock star, a blind inventor who helped advance the uses of nanotechnology and speech recognition. The latter is now used in various levels of government and for national defense. She's graced the covers of technical magazines, given speeches at MIT, Oxford, and U. C. Berkeley, and has set up various scholarship foundations. Quill was a mechanical engineer prior to Tessa's losing battle with congenital blindness. She was always at his elbow asking questions, taking apart radios, and any other household appliances she got her hands on and he would have to put back together. Fully without sight at twenty years old did not stop Tessa's inventiveness but then it was Quill at her side building out her ideas. With the advent of the Internet, Tessa immediately latched onto the idea of accessibility for the blind and speech recognition. They had been partners a long time before success and wealth came. But at the bottom of it all was the love that a father had for his daughters, something Tessa would sometimes forget when it came to business.

Tessa sprung to her feet. "This is the business, Quill! It's what we do now! You want to back up and keep making your little handicap devices, then fine. DO IT! But it was through *your* contacts that we got this contract in the first place! And now I'm delivering on it, so back off! Go away."

"Who do you think you are, speaking to *me* in that tone?" Quill remained seated but could not hide the hurt in his voice.

The gravity of Tessa's shame plopped her back down in her seat. "I'm sorry Dad."

"Now then, let's start again. Why?"

"No, you're right. I'm stuffing ten pounds of shit in a two-pound bag. I should have never brought this to Lorna's door, especially with Sally's history."

"Did you find out more?" Quill asked in even tones.

"Well, the Grandma did have a stroke and Sally did move her into that assisted living facility. Perez tracked her parents to New Zealand but it looks like they've moved again."

"No contact?" Quill pressed.

"Not that we're aware of. I'm tellin' ya', it's better to have no parents at all than—"

"No, it's okay." He assured her. "You know of what you speak. Are you still going to talk to her?"

"If I get a chance," Tessa replied.

"Well look, now, we don't know anything for definite. Officially, she was an aid worker in Bosnia and that's all. Her parents were the CIA agents. That doesn't mean she was, and I can't see why she would take that route in life. Anyway, what kind of CIA agent works as an *attorney* for Housing and Urban Development?"

"Do you think they made that report up?" After Lorna and Sally moved to California together and Tessa realized how serious their relationship had become, she had asked her CIA contacts to run a due diligence report on Sally. Nothing showed up, not even a traffic ticket, except the name change. Which led them to CIA's own files that had been made when Sally was doing aid work.

"No, I think it was a dangerous time and she was young and in a war zone. I think she probably has nightmares about it every night. She would never talk about it."

"Just playing devil's advocate here but, then, why would she have changed her name? She could be like a sleeper agent. You don't think they'd just let her walk away from killing a man in Bosnia do you?"

"I don't know. Just, when you talk with her maybe you could take a more concerned approach. She certainly shouldn't feel threatened."

"No, of course not. Lorna didn't mention anything? Like not even about the Grandma? She met her once, I know."

"She thinks the old girl's got dementia. Never said anything about the Grandfather helping start the CIA, nothing. I really don't think she knows anything about it."

"It's for the better. Could you imagine?" Tessa smiled.

"Yes!" Quill laughed for the first time today. "That's the problem."

Sally and Lorna sat at the kitchen table finishing off the soup. Sally dropped her spoon on the table. "It's like crack cocaine! I'm going to finish it off."

Lorna leaned back. "Go ahead. I've been eating it for two days."

Sally poured the rest of the soup into her bowl and used a piece of bread to sop up the remaining liquid in the pot before sitting back down and shoving the bread in her mouth. "So." She started chewing.

"Finish chewing," Lorna admonished. "So, yes, I think it's a bullshit excuse to divorce Annie. It's not like they were married at eighteen and became different people."

Sally nodded, continuing to chew.

Lorna added, "But when someone says, 'I just don't want to be married to you anymore', then what do you do? He's giving her the house, mind you."

"Whaa?" Sally tried to swallow.

"Yes, he said he wanted to keep making payments since it was a promise to her. Dude, he said he didn't want to break *that* promise."

Sally waved her spoon. "That sounds like guilt to me."

"I know. That's what I mean about a hoochie."

"No, I don't think it's a hoochie woman. We don't know what really goes on in a relationship. I mean *really*. Maybe Annie has a dark side. Maybe she's a Jekyll and Hyde."

"I agree. Some people are like that, but this is Annie we're talking about. Loyal, generous, uses color-coded paperclips?"

Sally nodded. "Yeah, it's Tim. But he's so – unimaginative. I think you have to have quite an imagination to have an affair."

"Really?"

Sally shrugged, "I guess, wouldn't you? To make all the justifications to yourself that it was okay." Sally paused and shook her head. "No, Tim's too 'by the book' for that."

"Ew, I just thought about something. What if Tim's had a secret life all along and now it's just too much to manage and he wants out. Like maybe he's got five kids somewhere. Or maybe he's a spy. You know, corporate espionage."

"Lorna! Tim is not a spy!"

"But he could be. His dad was a cop. They pass that shit through families."

Sally slapped her forehead with her palm. "You've got to stop. It's ridiculous."

"Well he's absolutely crushed Annie's spirit."

"That bad?"

"I think she's kind of in shock, really. She's blaming this job of his at Spectorgies, of course. And maybe she's right. I mean he spends over half his time working out of that Phoenix office."

"That's weird. Maybe *he's* the Jekyll and Hyde. So what's the plan?"

Lorna perked up. She'd been thinking the same thing. "The *plan* is to keep her busy. I thought about this when you were gone. Honestly, I was so busy and so tired at night I barely had time to miss you. Plus Tessa's coming and you know how she loves Annie."

"Mutual admiration society." Sally abruptly stopped eating when she heard several notes ring out an angelic melody and gently fade away.

"It's our new doorbell. Do you like it?"

"Where'd it come from?"

"The door."

"But where is it?"

"It's on the door."

"No, I'm asking where in the house is the sound coming from?"

"What's wrong with you? There's someone at the door pushing a little white button."

Sally leaned her head back and chuckled. "Okay."

The sound rang around the house again as Sally opened the front door. Roberta stood there looking around the front porch. "Where is that coming from?"

"I know. Lorna and her father did some renovations last week."

"I expected Saint Peter to open the door."

"Then come in." Sally moved away from the door and pushed her suitcase out of the way. "Lorna's dad was a mechanical engineer. I think that has a lot to do with it."

"Heading out?"

"Just getting back. I had to go see my grandma in Phoenix."

Lorna walked in from the kitchen area. "Hel-lo, Sergeant Fitzgerald."

Lorna and Roberta Fitzgerald are opposite sides of the same coin. Lorna with her classic blonde hair, blue-eyed features was stupefied when she met Roberta. Roberta, a black woman who easily cleared six feet, and as Lorna described her, was a Lena Horne look alike with a Foxy

Brown afro. Unfortunately, Roberta took Lorna's stupefaction the wrong way and feelings were hurt on both sides. It wasn't until Annie stepped in and told Roberta what glowing admiration Lorna had for her that Roberta took the extra steps to befriend Lorna. After all, it's not everyday someone believes you should have your own action figure.

"Not anymore. As of next week, it's Detective Sergeant Fitzgerald."

"That is fantastic news, Roberta." Sally patted Roberta. "Congratulations."

Lorna smiled but couldn't help but wonder.

Roberta answered the question, dancing across Lorna's expression.

"Keeling got a job in Concord. He's moving up to Captain."

Lorna nodded. "Good for you then. Can we get you something to drink?"

"No, no. I just stopped in to see if you've seen Tim around?"

Lorna and Sally exchanged a look.

Roberta caught the look. "What?"

Sally said, "We've not seen Tim in weeks. You know they're getting a divorce."

"What? Why?"

"We don't know," Lorna began. "He's either got a hoochie on the side or he's Mr. Hyde."

Roberta looked at Sally for clarification.

"Not even Annie knows why, or she's not saying."

Roberta rested her hand on her gun. "Huh. See, he called me a few days ago and asked me to meet him at the house and every time I drive by, his car isn't there. I guess I should call or stop in to see Annie."

Sally nodded. "That would be nice. But I would make it just a visit. I wouldn't bring up the divorce thing."

"No. Hey, you know what? I'm going to have to buy some clothes for this job. I've been wearing uniforms so long that I don't have any professional clothes. Where do you get your stuff?" Roberta waved her hand up and down Sally's tall body.

"When do you have time? There's a couple of shops in the city for tall women—"

"You could try the cross-dresser shops," Lorna helpfully added.

Roberta pursed her lips at Lorna. "Mmm, hm. You know my youngest son is still singing Diana Ross songs after your last babysitting adventure."

Lorna smiled. "He's a talented boy."

"I'm going to let you explain it to him then."

"Please! He's three and a half! It doesn't mean anything. When I was his age, I wanted to be a Charlie's Angel and I turned out okay."

Roberta turned to Sally, "So, this weekend?"

"Sure, Saturday or Sunday."

"Great. Oh, and speaking of Keeling leaving, we've got a new detective on the squad. He's, um…well, he's not like Keeling."

"Okay." Lorna was not getting the meta-message Roberta was sending her.

"You've built up a past with Keeling, bit of quid pro quo here and there. You have history with the department because of the incidents you helped out with on the island. But you know we've got this new guy in and he's really a taskmaster, letter of the law, and all that. We're all kind of starting out fresh."

Sally finally spoke up as she started seeing Roberta flail. "Don't worry. Lorna's got enough on her plate. She's not going to be getting involved with police matters. She's got her new self-help book out."

Roberta was grateful for the change of subject, "Oh that's great. What's it on, what's it called?"

"Nobody, *really*, likes you," Lorna smiled.

"It's satirical," Sally added.

Roberta thought for a moment, "Oh! You had me for a minute. Okay, I'll see you on Saturday then. And you," she pointed at Lorna. "When's that book go on sale, 'cause I got some people to hand that book to, right?"

"I'll let you know," Lorna nodded.

Sally closed the door behind Roberta. "What was that about?"

Lorna shook her head. "That, was a warning shot across the bough. I can't believe Keeling didn't stop in to say goodbye."

"Speaking of boughs," Sally wrapped her arms around Lorna's waist, "I haven't seen the bedrooms yet."

M. Saylor Billings

CHAPTER 2

THE AURORA SHIELD

Pearson Import, located on the seventh and eighth floor of 513 Market Street, has a stable business model. For twenty years they have made a slow but steady growth, but nothing so remarkable as to draw attention. They slowly expanded their offices from having one office to eventually occupying the entire seventh floor. Around October 2001 however, the company needed to expand their office space quickly and rented out the entire eighth floor. This action might have raised eyebrows, if Pearson Import actually existed as an import/export business.

NSA Special Agent Karen Bernard walked into her West Coast office on the seventh floor of 513 Market Street and plopped her bag down next to her chair. She looked at a file folder that had been neatly placed in the middle of her desk and groaned inwardly. "Chris! Get Donny in here!"

Karen picked up her phone to get her messages left for her during the night. Except for her eyes darting about the room, she stood motionless listening to the recordings. It was nothing but inter-office spam disguised as check in reports from her agents and rolled her eyes. What is it going to take to earn these guys' respect? Well, if they can't respect her, she thought, they might as well fear her. She went back down the hall and poured herself a cup of coffee.

As Karen returned to her office, Chris, the administrative assistant, looked up from her desk at the puffy circles under Karen's eyes. "Agent Bernard, is that coffee?"

Karen ignored the question. "I need you to pull together last night's reports from the three cases under our watch."

"I need you to drink tea, please."

Karen couldn't believe what she just heard.

"You have an annual physical again in a month. After your physical is over you may have more coffee. Tea is a pain to make so I will take charge of supplying it for you."

"I appreciate your concern but I'll be in charge of my physical well being, thank you."

Chris put a file back in her desk drawer and slammed the drawer shut. "Put it down," she smiled up to Karen. "One month, that's all I'm asking. Would you like a hard copy of the file as well?"

Karen watched another agent sidled into the break room. She took a deep breath and casually put the coffee down on Chris' desk. "Yes."

"I'll do that first and Donny's in your office now."

"Thank you." Karen shut the door to her office and sat down at her desk.

"Did you read it?" Donny asked, referring to the file on her desk.

"Why don't you tell me what it says?"

"Our informant is saying The Hayward made a second copy of the Aurora." Donny's grey eyes twinkled. The hair on the side of his head stood out revealing he hadn't showered this morning.

"You didn't think that was important enough to warrant a phone call?"

"I just found out three hours ago, at five o'clock this morning. I came in early to type this up so you'd have it first thing."

The only way Karen was going to get the agents assigned to her in line was to make a bad example of one of them. She needed to cut someone down and put them on a slow track to nowhere. Perhaps start a file and fire someone. Not this guy though. He had the untailored look of a guy who had pulled himself up from the dredges. Everything about him matched her preconceived notion of a NSA agent, except his lack of entitlement. Plus, he was too close to this case and frankly, she trusted him.

"But I thought this informant works for Spectorgies."

"He does. The Hayward contracted Spectorgies to handle their Human Resources."

"A shell game?" Karen used the short con game example once used to make quick money on the street using a pea and a walnut shell.

"Maybe. But we don't know what for."

"Do you know how much they contracted the H. R. for?"

"I'm working on that," Donny replied.

"I want to see that human resource contract. If The Hayward and Spectorgies are playing a shell game with us, we'll have go over any overlapping contracts. Where is this informant?"

"I don't know."

"What kind of proof does he have?"

"I'm not sure. Look, I tried calling his burner and it looks like he's disabled it. I've been trying to trace it though. I'm worried someone from The Hayward may have gotten to him and it's possible this is an erroneous report—

"Shoving a wedge between the NSA and Spectorgies," Karen nodded.

"—a wedge. Right. But if it's true, then both companies have committed treason."

"And do you actually think the United States is going put this on trial? One of the top defense companies, Donny?"

Donny shook his head. It was the first time that he noticed a light scarring across the brown skin of her neck.

Karen shrugged at him.

"How would you like me to proceed, ma'am?"

"Bring that informant in, Donny," Karen repeated herself. "It's better to have one man going down for treason, than a corporate defense partner."

There was a light tap at the door.

"Come in."

"Sorry. You left this on my desk, ma'am." Chris crossed over to Karen's desk and placed a steaming cup of tea down.

"Thanks. Sorry about that."

They waited a moment after Chris shut the door before proceeding.

Donny said, "So get the contracts and bring in the informant?"

"Yes, and get me this informants whole file."

"In the meantime, would you like me to put any feelers out to find out if it's true?"

"If it is true, then we will know soon enough." Karen grumbled.

"Don't you want to head that off? If word even gets out—"

"Donny, I agree with you. But this Spectorgies contract is so far above our heads so far up in the stratosphere where men play gods that we have no say in the matter. We make our reports, send them to the desk above us and let the matter play itself out."

"Okay, I agree. I get it. But just hear me out on a scenario?"

"Shoot."

"If, just *if,* we get bad news and Spectorgies got their hands on a copy of the Aurora, what would it take to get it back? Just one team. *Our team.* Would we need to go through search and seizure channels? If we can get our hands on the device, then no one is the wiser. It'd be like taking a knife away from a child. They've committed treason. Who are they going to complain too?"

"You want to do a black op?"

"Well, call it what you want."

What Karen wanted to do was crawl under her desk and take a nap. She lifted the tea and sipped. "Okay, let me read the report, bring the informant in and we'll go from there. Keep this under your hat, Donny. I don't want anything getting out until I take it upstairs."

"Got it. It may not work, there could be factors I'm not aware of—"

"Donny. Let me work it out."

"Sure." Donny got up to leave.

"Not a word Agent. Find that informant and as far as you know I'm making my report and sending it upstairs."

"Yup." Donny shut the door.

Karen opened the file on her desk and closed it. She leaned back in her chair considering what Donny had proposed. There wasn't a single agent under her command that she'd trust with a black op.

Without Joshua N. Edwards there would be no Spectorgies. He spent ten years in manufacturing, ten years in the financial sector, ten years in technology, and five years at the helm of Spectorgies. He still worked twelve to sixteen hours a day. The first woman he married for love. His second wife elevated his social stature. And this last one doesn't ask questions. Still in his workout clothes, he sat in the redwood-paneled office at his custom made desk flipping through the daily diary pages.

"Next week Tokuda, right." He punched a button on his phone. "Ace. Tokuda next week?"

"I'll bring in your file."

Edwards took the sweat towel and blotted his forehead. Rose Merkowitz walked in with a file and barely noticed him as she crossed to his desk. Aside from her reading glasses, she had hardly changed since she became his secretary at Kantor Capital twenty-five years ago. Her once-long flowing chestnut hair was now white and cut into a youthful bob. One time, many years ago, Edwards used her as a playing chip in a poker game. If he hadn't bluffed so well he would have lost her, a Mercedes, and twenty thousand dollars. He's called her Ace ever since.

"Where's that thing?" Edwards barked.

"The e-reader?"

"Where is it?"

"Mr. Bradshaw is loading it for you."

"With what?"

"He's downloading the newspapers and," she waved her hand, "the rest of the list you made."

"We're getting old, Ace."

"Speak for yourself. I do yoga now."

"With those hips?"

Ace picked up the file folder and smacked his arm. "Keep it up, Joshua Nelson, and I'll take early retirement."

"Good. I've been looking for a way to get rid of you." He yanked the file back from her.

"Please," Ace said, leaving his office.

"Fresh towels?"

"In your bathroom." Rose turned back at the door. "By the way you've got a couple of big mouths overseeing your special D section."

"What?" Edwards stood up.

"I'm having their personnel files brought up. You'll have my report on your desk."

"Can't you just fire them?"

"Above my pay grade."

Edwards let out his breath and wiped his forehead. "Where—?"

"You're not the only one who uses the Executive Gym, Mr. Edwards." Rose clicked her tongue and closed the door behind her.

At exactly two-thirty, Edwards sat at his oak conference table with two NSA section directors and Brian Hodge from The Hayward.

"No," Edwards was correcting Hodge, "if they were smart, they would have kept their mouths shut, right?"

The two section directors nodded in unison. Referring to the latest mapping software updates for which the NSA had contracted, the tall one said, "At any rate, cyber security is a team effort so we'd like to thank you guys for working together on this." Then he pushed his chair back from the desk and the shorter one followed. "Thanks for lunch."

"My pleasure," Josh smiled.

Both men left Edwards' office and shut the door. Edwards and Hodge sat back down.

Hodge spoke first. "Van Elder doesn't make social calls?"

Edwards frantically ran his hand around the chairs and under the tabletop where the two men had sat and then pushed the food cart with empty dishes out of the room.

"Can you take this, Ms. Merkowitz?" Hodge heard him say at the door.

Edwards calmly sat back down. "They bugged my office once."

"Sons-a-bitches." Brian would say anything to appease this man.

"Well, it's what they do. How's the human resource working out for you?"

"Great. Took a load off us, really. All that headhunting, hiring, firing, insurance - I was glad to source it out," Brian nodded.

"Good." Edwards chose his next words carefully. "We might actually have some further software needs for you guys."

Even though Brian was still new to dealing with conglomerate heads he knew exactly what Edwards was referring to. "We'd do what we could for you." This was what Brian had been working night and day for, a seat at the table with Spectorgies. This was where the real wealth was made through government, defense, and corporate contracts. Spectorgies was, in many ways, bigger than any of the intelligence agencies. They provided the modern tools the new world of spy craft hinged upon.

Edwards wanted a longer commitment from Hodges, besides the Aurora. "Cyber assets?"

An errant thought crossed Brian's mind. Was Edwards talking about disrupting power grids or protecting them? Brian pushed his lips out and nodded.

"I'm glad to hear it." Edwards tapped the arms of his chair and left the table.

Hodge took his cue and pushed back his chair. "Great lunch by the way."

Edwards strode over to his desk and pressed a button on the phone, "Ms. Merkowitz, could you bring Mr. Hodge his briefcase and coat?"

"Thanks for stopping by, Brian. We'll be in touch." Edwards stuck out his hand which Hodge shook.

Ms. Merkowitz opened the door, handed Brian his coat and briefcase. Brian smiled at her and felt the heft of his briefcase was about ten pounds lighter.

Edwards was pressing buttons on his phone already when the door shut.

"Morey, get the simulator ready. I'll be down in a half hour." He hung up the phone and pressed another button. "Abe, we're going to have to do some shuffling. We've got a big sale coming through. Bring me your brain and some financials at five o'clock."

Ace walked back in his office expectantly. He finally sat back down in his desk chair, "Cancel Tokuda," he said flatly.

"You can't."

"Why not?"

"Because they're filtering the Chinese. Don't piss them off Josh. They're a very touchy people."

He knew she was right but picked up the phone receiver and slammed it down out of frustration. "I have to get this thing out of here by next week at the very latest. Just go ahead and make some appointments over the weekend. Have the bidding on Monday."

"That's good. But I have my granddaughters Bat Mitzvah on Saturday."

"That's fine. Rebekah's twelve?"

"You donated to her college fund, generously."

"I'm glad. Okay, I'll have Morey then. I'll tell him when I go down to the simulator."

Rose handed him an Aurora brochure. "What do you think?"

Edwards gave the high gloss brochure a cursory glance and mumbled aloud, "Partnering with national...preserving freedom...protecting intelligence. Just add the solar part to this and it's fine, just not for the web."

She grabbed the brochure back from him and turned to leave.

"Hang on, Ace." Edwards stopped her. "Those two from section D. Where are they now?"

"Probably cleaning out there desks."

"Put them on the short list for operatives. Recommend them to the NRO or the NSA. Either one will do."

"The NRO," Rose said as she left the office.

Agent Todd Cassavetes looked Karen in the eyes and shrugged. "I'm sorry ma'am."

"Agent Cassavetes, you're telling me that you lost the entire file in a closed network and that it's irretrievable?"

"Ma'am, with all due respect, my specialty is field work if you would assign me a more suitable post—"

"Oh, I see, it's my fault. And due to your unbelievable failure to simply work through a case file, save it to a closed network and retrieve it when asked, you would like a promotion to a position that requires less oversight. That is an astounding request."

Todd opened his mouth to speak.

"Shut up. Here's what is going to happen, I'm going to file your cock up and your astounding request in your personnel record where I hope it will haunt you during your entire carrier. And for the foreseeable future you are on desk duty, in the pit. If you don't like that assignment, I invite you Agent Cassavetes, to find a new assignment in a different agency. I would be *happy* to provide you with a letter of recommendation."

Todd opened his mouth to speak again.

She pointed to her office door. "Now leave."

Todd got up and left.

Karen took a deep breath, turned off her computer and read Donny's report again. The Aurora cost the NSA ten million dollars. So, if there is a second one out there, it'll go for thirty or so, she thought. EarthSat seems to be in the clear. "Bunch of gear heads down there," she said aloud. But if it's Hayward's design, they could have cobbled together the hardware for this and basically just pulled in an engineer and a welder on the side. It's possible, but the real question is, did they sell it to Spectorgies? Van Elder, her division chief, had made a mistake by cutting out Spectorgies in this deal.

Karen was glancing through the pages of informant Tim Doughall's file when something caught her eye on the "Known Associates" page. She craned her head down and lifted the page up as her mouth fell open.

"No *fucking* way," she said aloud. She looked at the photo and the name again: Sally Thompson. She grinned. Funny, she thought, Sally Soucek didn't exactly seem like the marrying kind. What the hell is she doing out here? The last time she had heard anything about Sally Soucek was Sally had gone to law school. She flipped through the other pages of the file but, except for an address, there was no further information. Her mind wandered back to her CIA training in Bosnia with Sally and she shook her head. With Sally's family background, she could be the head of the CIA by now. Why would anyone throw all that away? So how much does Ms. Sally Do Good know about Tim's side gig with the NSA? Karen continued flipping through the file.

Chris' voice came through her phone. "Donny's here. Do you have a minute?"

"Sure." Karen pulled her feet off her desktop and sat up straight in her chair.

The door opened and Donny came in carrying a mug of coffee with Chris on his heels. "Do you need anything else tonight?" Chris asked Karen.

"No, I'm good. Thank you. Have a good night."

Chris glanced menacingly at Donny's mug of coffee and said, "You too," and shut the door again.

Donny sat down and lifted the mug to his lips and the door popped open again as he pulled the mug away from his mouth purposefully. Chris looked at them both for a beat then said, "Sorry, I put the daily in your draft folder on the server."

"Thank you," Karen smiled as Chris shut the door again.

Donny and Karen sat still facing each other for another moment before Donny put the coffee mug on Karen's desk.

Donny momentarily dispensed with professionalism. "Dude. One of these days we're going to find her body in the break room with tea bags shoved up her nose and that yoga mat shoved up her ass."

Karen nodded. "Coffee Nazi," and took a sip of the steaming brew. "Thank you."

Donny's eyes went to the files sitting out on Karen's desk. "So, what do you think, about my plan?"

Karen shut the files and nodded. "It is not a plan, it's a half baked idea." Karen smiled before continuing. "And I completely agree with you in principle. I think it would be cost effective and simple."

"But?"

"But. We have no proof. We can't just go in and smash and grab a Spectorgies outfit."

"The Hayward isn't Spectorgies."

"It doesn't matter. They are a working defense contractor. They don't operate under the same rules." Suddenly an idea flashed though Karen's mind, there was a time when she didn't operate under the rules either. There was no way this little shitty software outfit was going to put a wedge between the NSA and their number one supplier of people, arms, and information. And there was absolutely no way the NSA would do a black op mission against Spectorgies.

Donny watched the idea register on Karen's face. "What?"

Karen covered up for herself. "You seem pretty adamant about this. I think what you are saying is you'd like to go above my head. Am I right?"

Donny backed down, "No, Karen. I don't want to go above your head. Not at all."

She continued. "But look. If I *were* to put in my report addressing your suspicions and I can do that, mind you, one of two things will happen. It will be buried and we'll be put on some kind of hiatus from this case. Or, the chiefs upstairs will open a whole new case and you and I will not be a part of it. History has taught me that. But if I were to put in a report stating the facts regarding the various Spectorgies contracts with The Hayward and include this informants message, without any diagnosis or analysis then we can stay in the loop."

"Why?"

"Why what?"

"Why not put our ideas forward."

"At this stage we are not paid to think, and you'll get punished for it."

"Dude, that's bullshit. I'm sorry. But that's bullshit."

Karen smiled. "No, that's bureaucracy. You're going to have to learn how to walk this tight rope. You're a good agent and you very well may be right. But the boys upstairs want to feel in control. And it's part of your job to give them that."

Donny shook his head. "How long have you been doing this? How long have you worked for the NSA?"

Karen leaned back. "Let's see. I trained with the CIA back in Bosnia. Worked in Cuba, then the NSA picked me up. So almost twenty years."

"You must have started young."

Karen smiled. "Black don't crack."

Donny laughed. "You said that, not me."

"It's okay, it's true. So, write up your report again." Karen picked up the file and handed it back to Donny. "I'll put in my level of analysis and send it up. Okay?"

"Okay, but between you and me, we may be missing the boat here."

"Agreed. But let's follow procedure."

Donny got up and left the office closing the door behind him.

Karen rubbed her eyes. A plan was formulating in her head. If she were going to get her hands on that device, the Aurora, she would have to stay in the loop. No more playing grab ass with these little foot soldier agents like Todd, with their information hogging. Then she would have to get rid of that informant *and* she would need an escape route.

Josh Edwards stared at Morey in disbelief and tried in vain to keep his blood pressure down. The whirring of the machines in the Spectorgies lab wound down as Morey clicked away at the computer terminal in front of him.

"I believe the kids call it getting punk'd now, sir," Morey said with a balance of levity and concern.

Edwards lifted his eyebrows nodding and rubbed his forehead. "Punk'd? Is this a joke?"

"Nope. But the fact is that they loaded software for a video game, indicating it is a game to someone. Perhaps they see it as a joke or they have won something."

"Alright. So if we were dealing with professionals, they would have loaded it with software that *almost* works, right?"

"Yes. Their charade wasn't meant to go the distance."

"I still have a couple of days before the bidding."

"Do you want the engineers on deck for the weekend?"

"No. No we'll do the demonstration after the bidding. That will buy us time before the sale. So that would be Tuesday at the earliest." Edwards paused. "Where's the loophole in this?"

Morey shrugged. "I don't know. My guess is Hodge doesn't even know he gave you a fake. Unless it was planned before hand with the NSA."

"But that would mean he made a fake Aurora. You see what I'm saying? Were there three copies?" Edwards struggled with the idea.

"You mean, the real one, a copy for us, and a fake?" Morey shook his head.

Edwards was exasperated. "Would the NSA have him make a fake for someone? Why would he make a fake?"

"To sell to someone else, like someone who wouldn't know any better?" Morey guessed.

"Someone who wouldn't know any better, but wanted to be a player." Edwards nodded.

"Or someone could have made a swap and Hodge really doesn't know he had a fake one with him when he came to your office."

Edwards opened the door to the lab to leave and turned to Morey. "Set up a meeting with Hodges. That twit. Off site."

"Yes, sir."

CHAPTER 3

HURRICANE TESSA

Lorna didn't quite know what to say at this moment. She stood on Annie and Tim's front porch with the morning sun warming her back and her muted mouth slightly open. Annie stood opposite Lorna in the doorway slowly shaking her head side-to-side, tears streaming down her cheeks. Lorna took another moment searching her vocabulary for words to fill in the momentary beats that stretched into seconds. Annie had befriended Lorna the very first time Lorna stumbled upon this island. And during their various exploits together, no matter her personal cost, Annie spirit had never faulted. Lorna now witnessed as that spirit cracked and frayed.

She began slowly shaking her head in unison with Annie. Lorna couldn't believe her eyes. Annie, her little pillar of strength, had been abducted by aliens. And those aliens had put Annie into some kind of deconstruction toilet and flushed it! Annie's neat little auburn hair bob was streaked with some form of human liquid that also extended across her nose to her cheek and dried there. Her bloodshot eyes were crudded up puffy ping-pong balls of a nondescript color. Lorna smiled faintly. Annie smells like rotting fish.

"Okay," Lorna said, nodding and pushing her way inside, closing the door behind her. "First things first." Lorna was saying as she walked up the stairs to the master bathroom. Annie followed mindlessly.

"Now then," Lorna turned to her and said firmly, "I will bathe you if necessary."

Annie looked around despondently.

"Fine." Lorna started the shower and turned to disrobe Annie.

"I'll do it," Annie said regretfully.

"I'm going to go get you a towel and some fresh clothes." Lorna left the room while Annie disrobed.

When Lorna came back in, dispensing with any respect for privacy, she pulled the curtain back and handed Annie a washcloth. "Use plenty of soap. I left your clothes on the counter."

Lorna moved around in high gear, changing Annie's bed linens and collecting the dirty clothes strewn on the floor before returning downstairs. She tossed the soiled wad into the laundry room.

She continued the breakneck pace in the kitchen and living room. She grabbed a trash bag and filled it with the boxes of food, left over plates, empty wine bottles, scraps of *whatever that was*, and dropped the bag on the back porch. As she finished the kitchen, two little furry heads popped around the corner. Lorna was allergic to Bert and Ernie, Annie's Australian shepherds, but she smiled at them just the same. She found the dog walker's number on the refrigerator and called it.

"Hi, this is Lorna Tollison, Annie Doughall's friend? Annie just got her divorce papers. Can you come by today and take the boys out, maybe to the dog park? I think it's been a couple of days for them...that would be fine. I'll leave a key and some cash in the back porch planter for you. I'm kidnapping Annie for the day...no, I insist. You're doing me a big favor by coming by at such short notice...Thank you so much."

She sat at the kitchen table sorting Annie's mail as Annie crept into the kitchen.

"Feel better?" Lorna asked.

"No."

"But you smell so much better. I can't believe you had this *epic* pity party and didn't invite me! I feel like Cinderella, here. Hungry?"

Annie looked around the clean kitchen as if she'd never seen it before. "No."

"Looks like you got the bad news today," Lorna said, pointing to the divorce papers on the table. "Annie, do you have a lawyer?"

"We're not using one. We did it on the internet."

"Um. Okay. But would you mind if Sally looked over this for you guys?"

"Yes. I would," Annie snapped and snatched the papers out of Lorna's hands.

Lorna nodded in mock understanding. "So, instead of having a close family friend, who happens to be an attorney, make sure you two aren't screwing up both your lives, you'd rather take your chances. That's some sound thinking."

Annie grabbed the rest of her mail away from Lorna. Bert and Ernie poked their heads in again. "I have to take the dogs for a walk. And I'd like a little privacy, thank you."

"I called Angela the dog walker for you. They're going on a play date to the park. I've set it all up already."

"Oh—" Annie opened her mouth to yell and protest.

"So here's the thing." Lorna went on, "I think you must be going through hell. The rug has been yanked out from under your feet. And eventually time will work it's magic and you might start feeling better. But," Lorna paused for effect, "you are not alone. Just for a little while, why don't you let Sally and I help out? You need to be kept busy and I've got just the cure."

"What?" Annie wanted to know. Maybe it was drugs.

"Tessa."

"Oh, I like Tessa. Why didn't you tell me she was coming?"

"I am. She'll be here, like, now."

"Oh, maybe she'll send me to Paris," Annie thought out loud.

Lorna blinked. "Well, you can ask her. When was the last time you did any work?"

Annie worked at home for an online marketing group, but considering the state of the house, Lorna was worried she wasn't keeping pace with her workload.

"Oh, yeah. Nooo," Annie whispered.

"Annie, I need you to turn off your emotions for, like, an hour. Remember that time we were in that fire and you didn't panic? You just got down and pulled that woman out to safety. I need that Annie back for a little while. I need you to send in a family emergency notice or what ever you do to get some time off. Then, I need you to come over to my house." Lorna lifted the divorce papers off the table. "I'm taking these for Sally to look through, this is no time for – whatever reason you have for privacy." Lorna walked over and started the dishwasher. "Okay, we good? Come on, let's go back into your office."

Annie followed Lorna into her office and sat down at the computer. "What do I say?"

"You have a private family matter and will be available next week."

Annie giggled aloud.

"Oh my goodness, look at that." Lorna pointed at the ceiling. "A dark cloud is passing."

"You're ridiculous, you know that?"

"Hurry, I'll put the load of sheets and towels in," Lorna threw over her shoulder as she left.

The first time Tessa flew to Oakland Airport by herself it was such an utter disaster for the airport personnel that they now go on high alert when they see her name on the passenger rosters. Granted, it was only one man's fault for leaving her on the motor trolley while he took his break for a half hour. At any point she could have gotten off the trolley and found her way to help. But, who leaves a blind woman stranded in a strange airport?

"I prefer to walk, if that's okay," Tessa said to the squeaky soprano who greeted her.

"Absolutely, I'll walk with you. I really dig your glasses." The young security guard, Amber, seeing Tessa did not carry a cane, put her elbow out and stood next to Tessa. To Amber's shock, Tessa just started walking forward.

"Thanks. I was feeling very Carol Channing this morning."

"Chanel," Amber corrected her and caught up to Tessa's pace.

Tessa smiled passively. "Yes. Chanel. Carol Chanel." Tessa changed the subject. "Any changes to the airport lately?'

"Just the new artwork on the walls. Every year there's a theme and then every few months they'll change out the installations. "

"What's this year's theme?"

The security guard quickly realized that Tessa was being guided by her own voice and she should begin talking about what they were passing by as they walked. "Environment. They had a contest for school children and the winners had their drawings put up."

"Oh, good for them," Tessa said pleasantly as they made their way to the baggage claim.

From the bottom of the escalator, Sally could see Tessa's screaming red hair before she could actually see her whole body. She smiled up at the airport security guard who leaned over and said something to Tessa. Tessa waved down in Sally's general direction as they descended.

Sally smiled and nodded. Tessa was wearing her button pin that read: I'm not deaf.

When they disembarked the escalator, Tessa put her hand out. "Thank you, Amber."

The young security guard beamed. "It was my pleasure. Do you need help with your bags?"

"No, we'll get them," Sally said.

Amber hustled off - she just *had* to tell someone.

Sally and Tessa embraced. "How was your flight?"

"A little bumpy. But ya' know, I think it's always bumpy coming out here."

"Depends on what time of year too, I think."

"Can you show me to a bathroom?" Tessa asked.

Tessa took a step forward but adjusted her direction to Sally's voice. "I can. I should go too. And I brought you some water while we wait for your bags," Sally said as they entered the woman's restroom.

She tapped Tessa's shoulder to stop. "On the right, papers on the left, automatic flushers." And showed herself into the stall next to Tessa.

When they sat down across from the baggage carousel Tessa began, "I wanted to talk to you about something." She paused. "I just don't know the, well, I'm not sure how to go about this now that I'm here."

Sally gave a nervous giggle. "Sounds ominous. Start with 'Once upon a time.'"

"I know your history," Tessa blurted out. "Even your real last name. It's So-sick."

"It's pronounced Soo-check," Sally calmly corrected her. But a pain shot through Sally's chest so sharp that she almost doubled over. The jig was up, her worst fear realized. Everything she's worked so hard to make for herself, gone. Tessa's lips were moving but Sally could only hear her own heart beat under the hum of white noise.

"I don't care. I mean, I don't care about the past. I've known you now a long time and I've figured you've had your reasons for all of it. I think you must have changed your last name and moved the minute you had your chance, when your parents died," Tessa explained.

"I did," Sally snapped back to the moment. "I don't care about the past either. What I care about is here and now. And *you're* not going to screw it up for me. You have no idea what I've been through or how hard I've worked to get away from all of that." Sally's voice was rising.

Tessa reached her hand out and touched Sally's arm, her skin was clammy. "Sally, calm down. Did you hear what I said? I'm on your side. I want to help."

"I don't need your help."

"Okay, but just calm down, please. Do you know where your parents are?"

"How the hell should I know? They're probably dead."

"No, they aren't."

"How do you know?"

"I know."

"Whatever." Sally got up and walked away leaving Tessa sitting at the airport baggage carousel.

"Not again." Tessa adjusted herself to face forward in her seat. She sat for a few moments deciding whether or not to pull out her cell phone and call Lorna or just catch a cab.

Finally, she heard Sally's voice again. "Orange. Right?"

"Yes. Thank you." Tessa held out her hand and Sally placed a bottle of Orange soda in it.

"Look, don't say anything to Lorna. I will tell her." Sally sat back down, her voice was commanding, there was none of its usual laissez faire bounce to it.

Tessa noted the significant change in the quality of Sally's voice and wondered about the personality behind it. She knew a lot about people by their voices. The dialect and the language they choose, the tension in the vocal chords, the pitch at which they delivered requests and commands. Sally's voice suddenly had the cold New England clip to it. Tessa needed to keep the conversation going. "Why? I mean, why would you do that? I don't plan to tell her. Quill certainly doesn't plan on it."

"Quill knows?"

Tessa modulated her own voice into a comforting nonchalance. "He doesn't care. You're part of his *brood*. He worries something might come back on you," Tessa lowered her voice, "and you know what I'm talking about."

"It's not. Wait, how did you find out?"

"I've got high level defense contracts. You don't think they did background checks?"

Sally shook her head and took a swig of soda.

"What kind of name is Soucek?" Tessa tried a different tactic.

But Sally didn't back down. "Tessa, I don't know. I don't even know what their real first names are. They may have said it once, but I don't know."

"Okay. Well, don't worry about Quill. All he cares about is future grandchildren."

Sally took another swig. "I'm third generation murders on one side, God knows what's on the other….probably opium smugglers."

"Well, don't look at me. I've got congenital blindness. You think I want to pass this shit on?"

"Why are you telling me this?" Sally demanded.

"Because I've known, for a while, and it just felt wrong not to say anything. And you're family so I don't….I just think that you've probably had to shoulder a lot by yourself on this and I want you to know you don't have to anymore."

"I appreciate that, Tessa. But no, that's over and I'm enjoying my life just fine. Nothing's coming back on me."

"Can I ask you something though?"

"What?"

"Are you still working for the CIA?"

"No. I work for HUD. I'm a desk jockey. Happily ever after, a desk jockey."

"Okay. It's kinda cool though, to have a trained killer for a sister in law."

Sally inhaled deeply. "That's not true either. That's exactly why I don't want Lorna to know. I have enough problems with Lorna's vigilante nature. God knows what she'd fell entitled to do if she knew."

"Well, we're in agreement with that."

The conveyor belt squeaked and the baggage carousel moaned alive. Sally stood up to walk over to the side but Tessa tugged on her arm again.

"Did a package come for me yesterday?"

"No, I didn't see anything. Lorna didn't say anything."

"I was afraid of that, isn't the EFS delivery, don't they have a distribution center near you?"

"It's on the way."

"Do you mind if we stop on the way home?"

"No, that's fine."

Annie had made it back over to the house just in time. Lorna had been prattling on non-stop, pulling Annie out of her melancholia, so they almost didn't hear the front door shut.

Sally and Tessa walked in just as they were setting the kitchen table. "I'm here!" Tessa yelled.

Sally smiled as Lorna squealed. It's going to be a loud week, Sally thought.

"We're sorry we're late. Sally got lost."

"I did not," Sally defended herself, the bounce returning to her voice. "Tessa made us stop over at the EFS distribution center—"

"I sent you a package," Tessa cut her off.

"Yeah, it's right here, it came on the morning drop, I was over at Annie's," Lorna said.

"Oh good. Well, we'll get to that later," Tessa said.

"Do you want to have lunch or see the house first?" Lorna asked.

Annie and Sally exchanged a questioning look.

"Oh see the house, of course. But it smells wonderful."

"I baked a chicken," Lorna said proudly.

"For lunch? I was thinking tuna salad or something light."

Lorna and Tessa wandered arm in arm into the front living room as Sally and Annie fell back and went into the kitchen.

"You look great," Sally said.

"I feel like I've been run over by a train," Annie replied.

Sally saw a manila envelope on the kitchen counter and only need to glance Tim's familiar signature in the corner. She knew instantly what it contained and swept it off the counter and placed on the top of the refrigerator. "I'll look that over tonight."

Annie dropped her head. "Thanks."

"Well," Sally said. "I have good news and bad." And pulled out a couple of food containers from the refrigerator.

"Oh Sally, I don't think I can take it."

"The bad news is, Lorna has made you her mission."

"Oh, no."

"The bad news is, she'll probably get her sister to help."

"What's the good news?"

"I speak to you as a survivor. Let me advise you in this journey you are about to take. Don't fight it. Just agree and move on."

"Okay. Thanks."

They both jumped when they heard squeals coming from Lorna's office. When they got to the door Lorna was on all fours on her desk, laughing. And Tessa, the *renowned blind inventor*, was doing a headstand in Lorna's reading chair.

"What happened?" Sally searched the room.

Tessa flipped herself back onto the floor. "This isn't an office of a novelist, it's the office of a lunatic!"

Annie looked up at Sally. "We better get that chicken out."

Sally agreed and followed Annie. "Poor Quill, can you imagine raising them?"

Despite Lorna and Sally's objections, Patience sat in Tessa's lap all through lunch. Occasionally she would hold a piece of chicken in her hand for him to nibble on. The two of them had some kind of strange bond that Sally wouldn't question, but Lorna did.

"You're spoiling him," Lorna said.

"So? What's he gonna do, grow up and be a drug dealer?" Tessa countered.

Annie giggled. "Or a broker."

"What about Fortitude?" Lorna asked.

"Maybe he's wandering around that Escher painting of an office dad built." Tessa paused. "But, I'll make it up to him. He can sleep in my bed."

Sally slapped her forehead in exasperation.

Tessa put her fork down and Patience leapt from her lap. "Lorna." Tessa started but stopped and made several hand gestures to her.

Sally and Annie watched the sign language with some fascination.

Lorna turned to Sally and said accusingly, "What'd I tell you? Huh? When you called from Phoenix?"

Sally was dumbfounded. What had she told her? Sally's mind raced.

Lorna filled in the blank, "Cagey!" and pointed to Tessa. She got up and grabbed Tessa's purse and shoved it in Tessa's hands.

"I don't understand what's happening." Annie admitted.

Tessa dug around her purse. "It's a game we played when Lorna was little."

"Helen Keller." Lorna finished Tessa's thought. Eyebrows raised and Lorna reluctantly explained, "I didn't completely understand the blind thing and I had read a book on Helen Keller and then I found a book on sign language."

Tessa found what she was looking for and held up a set of keys, she lifted the key fob and pressed it. Suddenly a low hum began vibrating around the house.

"How do you play, Helen Keller?" Sally asked.

"Why do you have car keys?" Annie asked Tessa at the same time.

"Is that what those are?" Tessa said. "I thought they were house keys."

Lorna sat back down.

Annie leaned over to Tessa's keys. "Well yeah," Annie looked closer at them. "I guess they are."

"Excuse me!" Lorna said. "What the hell is that?"

Tessa leaned forward. "Please don't be mad, Lorna, I had Dad install a frequency jammer with your doorbell. I need it for when I visit."

"Okay that's fine. I don't care, but he did it in secret? Why would he do it in secret?"

Annie's eyes were twitching between the sisters now. She recognized the fuse to Lorna's outrage had been lit.

Sally pushed herself away from the table. "I'll get the Jell-O." She was taking cover.

"How would he do that, huh?" Tessa countered.

Lorna's voice rose, "He could have wrote a note. He could have told me the countless times we were at the hardware store. He could have showed me how it worked. Pick one. No secrets, right?"

Sally heard that last bit from the kitchen and rolled her eyes.

"Dad did this at my request. I've got several contracts worth worrying about right now and I'd like to come to see my sister and speak freely. I don't want to worry about if someone's using a big ear to listen in on me. So, I'm sorry I didn't tell you about it earlier. I'm sorry okay? But you know now and you know why. Dad felt bad, I know, we had argued about it. He probably felt guilty and left it up to me to tell you. And he's not wrong about that, really."

Annie watched them carefully, she couldn't peel her eyes away as Tessa diffused the Lorna bomb. Finally, she spoke up. "What's a big ear?"

"It's slang for a listening device," Lorna said. "You know those things you see in football games, where guys are holding like a dome thing with a metal pole sticking out or them middle. It's like that."

Sally came back in with four cups of cherry Jell-O. "So, what do you want to talk about?" Sally asked.

"No a better question is what else did you have installed?" Lorna wanted to know.

Tessa took a deep breath, "The paint he used contains an aluminum iron oxide, and it blocks your RF signals."

"Ho-ly shit," Sally said.

"Wow." Annie's face brightened.

Lorna leaned back in her chair. "Tessa, what have you gotten yourself into? Why are you here?"

"It's business. Using nanotechnology I built a small piece, like the size of a wallet, that would capture wi-fi and radio, RF signals and relay that into any network."

"Whoa." Annie sat up. "What?"

"You know how we connect to the internet through an Ethernet cable and then we put a wireless router on it for wifi around the house? That's called a LAN –local area networks. But there are WAN's, wide area networks, CAN's, campus area networks, MAN's, metropolitan area networks, right?"

All three women nodded and Tessa didn't hear any dissent.

"Okay, well this little doodad doesn't need permission to join the networks, it's like a cockroach. I considered calling it 'la cucaracha'. It uses relay's to piggy-bag on any network, anywhere, undetected. No satellite pinpointing. And I had David, who builds audio interfaces for me develop the audio nanotechnology for it. I'm meeting him here. I sent him a text when I found out you didn't receive the package."

"When?" Sally asked.

"You were in the distribution center. I have an audio interface on my phone."

"Wait," Lorna was catching up. "So you could effectively download something secure and move that information somewhere else without getting traced."

Annie's mind raced to the logical conclusion. "Ho-ly crap. You could take information from banks or government servers, alter the data, and reload it to the servers. That's hacking. You just made hacking commonplace." Annie added sardonically, "Hey let's all go to the coffee house and fill our bank accounts? Tessa, just because you can, doesn't mean you should."

"It gets worse."

"*How*?" Sally cried out.

"If I'm not mistaken, it was stolen from that package I sent you."

Lorna momentarily lost her mind. The colorful tapestry of obscenities she wove included actual words in several languages but the taboo gestures she employed in staccato measures added a frame and dimension to her freak out which elevated it to an Old Testament proportional epic. Tessa waited patiently for Lorna to either pass out from lack of oxygen or her senses to return to her, the former being the most likely. Sally, on the other hand, was having a really bad day and she would like to go to bed now. But Annie enjoyed these moments of hysterics, one day she'd like to video one of Lorna's fits and put it to music.

Lorna sat back down. "Well?"

Tessa took her glasses off. "I'm sorry was there a question in there?"

Annie choked and water shot out her nose. "I'm sorry." She stumbled off to the kitchen to clean up.

"As I was saying, they won't get too far with it." Tessa took off her I'm not deaf button and turned it over in her hand. "I took out the memory chip. I also know who stole it."

"So, what are you going to do?" Sally asked.

"I'm going to steal it back," Tessa said.

CHAPTER 4

THE AULD ALLIANCE

Michael Chan had only met Christy Booth in person one other time. It was right after he had been recruited by the FBI "special" fraud division, and survived the boat blast in the Ohlone estuary that killed his new trainer. Before that night Michael had been an IT guy, a button pusher who worked in the FBI's cyber forensic unit in the San Francisco office. He still thought of himself as an IT geek, complete with the Blue-ray *Star Wars* commemorative box set edition and plastic light saber. His daydreams of casting himself as the Chinese Luke Skywalker or even R2D2 still got him through the rough times. But he never wanted to be Hans Solo or Lando Calrissian, dabbling in treachery.

But here he is, a covert agent going to a covert meeting, and who knows, maybe it is in a covert restaurant and Jabba the Hut will be holding court in the back room. He never asked to be assigned to this "special" fraud division. It is "special" because it is headquartered out of Virginia and works independently from other West Coast units. He investigates any and all fraud cases he can gin up or lay his hands on and turns them in to the San Francisco fraud division as a cover for the Virginia team's "unofficial" and nefarious activities. The irony that there was a "special" fraud division being fraudulent in their activities under cover of the FBI's fraud division made Michael smile inwardly.

In his capacity as a "special" agent out of the Virginia office, however, he worked in the shadows now. He collected information, distributed disinformation, and dipped a fateful finger into corporate espionage cases that could or would never be brought to trial.

A meeting with Christy Booth was indeed rare. Michael had worried about it the entire drive from San Francisco to Los Angeles. In their first meeting, Christy had warned him about the San Francisco fraud division boss, Wayne Felding. Apparently, Wayne had a chip on his shoulder. Michael was to guard himself against Wayne's meddling and attempts to bring Michael's "special" status into question. But that turned out not to be the case. As a matter of fact, he hadn't seen much of Wayne. Any fraud case Michael pulled in to Wayne's division was executed, processed, and prosecuted without additional questioning from Wayne.

What crossed Michael's mind now, as he made his way to the door of the Chinese restaurant in Los Angeles, is that Christy must know he was in the middle of a huge case. Why pull him in right now? over five hundred miles away from his informant?

Christy sat chatting with the waitress as Michael approached the booth.

"Ni Hao," Michael said.

"Ni Hao," the waitress said and left the booth giving Michael room to sit down.

"I hope you don't mind. I really wanted some good home cooked food." Christy tapped the table next to her disassembled cell phone.

Michael smiled and pulled out the battery from his cell phone as well. "I never turn down a good meal. You speak Chinese?"

"I do, and Farsi and Finnish."

"Finnish? At what point did you feel Finland was a threat to national security?"

"It was a phase I went through in college." Christy smiled.

Michael waited patiently for Christy to assemble her thoughts. She had lost some weight since their first meeting in that farmhouse in Virginia where he also met the directors of the special fraud division, Frank Danvers and Elliot Pickles.

"How's Elliot?" Michael asked.

Christy ran a hand over her close cropped hair and took off her oversized black-framed glasses. "He died. In his sleep, it was peaceful at least."

"I'm sorry. I know he was your mentor."

"Yes, well. He was lucky. He had an advanced stage of liver cancer too."

"Well, should I do anything? I mean—"

"No. It was all prearranged. You know Elliot, no stone left unturned. Frank and I have been scrambling around, notifying our units. But he had this case of yours all mapped out for us," Christy explained.

"Well, I didn't hear from you after my last drop so I was surprised you called this meeting. I have to tell you, it's kind of a bad time to be doing this. I left my informant in a safe house."

"That last drop was a doosey, it's why I'm here. You're going to have to dump that informant, hard and fast. We found out that Spectorgies put the Aurora copy up for sale already. Which means they either haven't put it in their little simulator yet or have absolutely no idea what to do with it."

"Maybe the NSA is trying to lure someone out of their shell using Spectorgies and the Aurora as bait? Maybe Russia or even some arms dealers," Michael guessed.

"No. Elliot would have known about that. But does Spectorgies know they got the fake and there is another one loose out there? I'm worried about the implications of making the fake. In other words, maybe it would have been better just to have had it stolen."

"All they have to do is ask Hodges and they'll know the copy *was* stolen."

"Did your informant know who his counterpart was?"

"No, I used one of my IT agents, Sunil, at The Hayward but he's out now. They had him working on some mapping project so he had some room to get to know the players. He got away with it but by now they'll know he had something to do with it. Hopefully, that'll throw some confusion around Tim, the informant."

"How'd you pull that off? Under Wayne?"

"Wayne doesn't talk with me much. You know that heads up you and Elliot gave me about him being a buttinski didn't pan out. Honestly, he couldn't care less about my operations."

Christy leaned back in the booth and crossed her arms with a harrumph. "That's strange. I'll have to look into old Wayne. But this is unbelievably huge, Michael. To have our little unit get the drop on the NSA? I wish Elliot could have lived to see it."

Tim took his shoes off and rubbed his feet and looked around the dilapidated apartment. He could see the red neon 'Lemon Sud' sign reflecting onto the ceiling from his sleeping bag. The rush of stealing a ten million dollar satellite device for the FBI was wearing off and leaving him somewhat empty. He would really like to see Annie about now. He wanted to talk with her, tell her the importance of what he's doing and that she won't have to work with those people she hates anymore. He checked his watch again. It had been three hours and thirty-two minutes since Michael left. What the hell kind of errand did Michael run? Tim's mind flashed back to his former handler, the one blown up on that boat. Then Michael shows up and he's so new he still had his new agent smell about him.

Tim put his shoes back on. The consequences of what he had done were beginning to sink in. What if Michael was playing him? Setting him up to take a fall. Then the FBI's hands would be clean, they wouldn't have anything to answer to the NSA about. Michael and the FBI never did find out who blew that boat up. Tim got a wrenching feeling in his gut. He really hadn't taken any real precautions. Now he's just here like a sitting duck. Tim got up and paced. Something was wrong. Michael shouldn't be away this long. If something has happened to Michael, Tim thought, he might very well be in danger too. He needed a plan B, and some type of insurance at the very least. He paced around looking for something, anything. He went to the door of the apartment to leave but stopped. He turned and went back for the Aurora copy and key to the van. With any luck Annie will be out or over at Lorna's house.

The waitress returned with a small teapot and water's for them both. "I ordered us spicy salt prawns, chow fun and fish, how's that sound?" Christy said.

"It's fine," Michael said looking around the empty restaurant. "I hope you don't mind, but have you lost some weight?"

Christy smiled. "Baby weight."

"Oh that's right. You had that baby. Now I remember."

"I'm surprised. Elliot had you so cooked."

Michael grimaced, remembering his wounds from the boat blast and the old doctor who patched him back up.

"Well, it was that doctor he used, that veterinarian. He probably pumped you with horse speed."

Michael looked behind him again.

"Expecting someone?"

"No. Look, I need to get this over with," Michael explained.

"Okay."

The waitress set the prawns and an assortment of appetizer dishes on the table. And walked away again.

"Is there any way the NSA can link this to us?" Christy asked.

"No. Like I said, I only used Sunil and the informant."

"And Sunil?"

"He's a hundred percent. If I was ever allowed to expand my operations I would put Sunil in for a transfer."

"Okay. The NSA and Spectorgies swap out employees on a regular basis. When you drop that informant, Spectorgies might suspect the NSA had something to do with it. As a matter of fact...." Christy paused and ate a prawn. "I've got a better idea," she mumbled out, chewing quickly. "If we *make* him disappear, they would definitely suspect the NSA. It'll be enough of a wedge to drive in between them to slow down Spectorgies operations."

"What do you mean, disappear?"

"Michael, he's an informant. He's done. He's definitely done at Spectorgies and if those monkeys at The Hayward ever put two and two together, he could be *done for*."

"Christy. I thought you said we didn't do violence."

"What are you talking about? I don't mean *kill* the guy. I have an idea how to make him go away for a while though, at least. This is actually turning out better than Elliot could have imagined. If people think this device is on the open market, *we* could lure a lot of these assholes out of hiding."

"Do you know who's stepped forward to buy yet?"

Christy shook her head no and took a swig of her tea. "They had bidders lined up five minutes after they had a lunch with the NSA." Christy giggled a little. "What a bunch of assholes," and then fell into a heaving laughing fit ending with a sigh. "Oh, I love my job sometimes. Can you believe those greedy bastards? They sign a contract with the NSA under the super-duper top secret guideline, then they have the balls to have a duplicate made to sell to our enemies on the side?" She stabbed another prawn.

"What'll happen to them?" Michael asked.

"Nothing." Christy shrugged. "They really are above the law. That's why you and I have this job, I might add. The Defense Department is so reliant on them, there is nothing to be done, really. We just have to try to thwart any serious wrongs they may be tempted to do."

"What's it worth? A cloaking device like the Aurora, I mean."

Christy chewed and look around before answering. "To the U.S., I think it was about ten mill. But on the open black-market thirty at least. If it works as promised then it will be the only one of its kind, so maybe more."

"Okay, so when do you want to take the delivery from me?"

"A week or so. Let everyone get good and panicked about it so we have breathing room. I'm going to have Frank put Sunil in for special training, get him out of there for a month or so. Does he know how to speak Chinese?"

"I don't think so."

"Good. Elliot—"

The waitress came back with dishes of noodles and fish. She placed plates in front of them both and placed the side dishes around them. "More tea?"

"Could I have some iced tea?" Michael asked.

"Wait, are you teaming Sunil with me? I still have that Chinese thing that's been brewing. If I go in with that, I'm going to need someone on the outside."

"We don't work that way. Michael, I was in the field for 8 years by myself, in *Boston* no less. Elliot didn't set the program up like that. It's one person, one town, and an ass-load of informants. Cops, civilians, park rangers, fire fighters, those are your best allies. But hey, look -- you're bringing in a HUGE fish, practically a coup d'etat. Maybe Frank has different plans for future operations, especially if the cyber world keeps heating up at this pace."

"But what I'm saying is I didn't do it by myself. It really was that informant. His name is Tim."

"That's why you have the mother of all slush funds. I'll bet the only reason that informant stayed with the FBI and didn't switch his allegiance to the NSA was for the cash. That's how these informants work; they just go to the highest bidder. But we may not have to dig too deep into that just yet. Before Elliot died, he made contact with this couple that worked as a team during the seventies and eighties for the CIA. Apparently they had all met years ago back when Elliot was working in Ireland, before he went, well, underground. But Elliot was dead before they had a chance to meet again, but then they showed up at his gravesite. How did they even know he died? And where he was to be buried?"

Michael shrugged. How should he know?

"So Frank meets with them and it turns out the old man was the one who pulled Elliot from that car bomb in Ireland, and they've kept in touch through the years, exchanging information and whatever."

"Christy, I have a *six* hour drive ahead of me."

"Relax. This is worth it. So there's Frank wondering just what the hell Elliot meant to contact these two for, right? And it turns out they were heading to your neck of the woods up there."

"San Francisco?"

Christy nodded.

"What would the CIA have to do with San Francisco? I mean, was he sending them out for this?"

Christy continued chewing and shook her head.

Michael put his chopsticks down and thought for a long minute. Who does he know who is retired from the CIA? Christy watched with some anticipation. Somehow that rang a bell for him. Finally, a faint memory of his first meeting with Elliot. Then the memory became more clear with his first meetings with Tim. And then it dawned on him. "Oh. My. God."

"Small world, ain't it?" Christy popped a prawn in her mouth.

Brian Hodge clicked his cell phone off and tossed it on the couch. What could Edwards possibly want now? Edwards practically strong-arms him into making a copy of the Aurora and then showers him with money. And now he wants another meeting, for what? Thinking back now, it was the way Edwards said 'Cyber assets' that didn't ring true somehow. Cyber assets could mean anything. Brian took a long pull off his joint. The language in the contract between the NSA and The Hayward said the Aurora was for the exclusive use of the NSA. It didn't say he couldn't make a copy and sell it to Spectorgies. Technically he didn't do anything wrong. It was just good business and it got his foot in the door with these big contracts. If he had sold it to anyone but Spectorgies, he'd be worried. Why was he worried about this? It was done. Money in the bank and more to come.

If anything, he should be worried about manpower. He'll have to give that human resources guy a call again and bring in some more coders, hopefully, some who bathed regularly. Going corporate means he'll have to do some house cleaning with the staff, as well. He'll have to hire some secretaries, bring in some suits, and stop using that temp service. If The Hayward becomes the go-to cyber asset resource for Spectorgies, there is no telling how exponentially his company could grow. Not bad for a scrawny kid from Oakland, he told himself as he finished the joint and stabbed it out.

Michael stopped for gas just before entering the Grapevine corridor on I-5 and picked up two packets of energy pills. The soundtrack to *Beauty and the Beast* was on sale at the counter. He bought that too -- he would need something irritating to help fight off sleep as he drove. But the entire ride back to Oakland, he went over and over his conversation with Christy. He was very concerned as to just how flippant Christy had been about the disposability of his informant. Tim was a valuable asset. More than that, he was trustworthy and perched right there in the heart of most of their target cases.

The words to the soundtrack stayed with him as he walked a circuitous route through the streets of Ohlone Island. He rounded the corner onto the Island's shopping district, to a street more aptly named for a village in England, High Street. It was still the wee hours of the morning for this sleepy suburb but he could see lights on and movement in back of the new Auld Alliance Cafe. He continued down the street as the streetlamps flicked on and off and he took a right on a side street to the Lemon Sud. Michael gave three knocks paused and then another sharp one before letting himself into the squalid safe house apartment.

Tim came out of the bathroom. "What the fuck?"

"I'm sorry," Michael said wearily.

"I was just about to take off, man."

"I don't blame you."

"What the hell is going on? Is it clear for me to head back to Phoenix or not?"

Michael shook his head and looked over Tim's shoulder. "Any coffee?"

"Fuck you!"

"What's with the hostility?"

"You said, 'Wait right here, I'll be back,' like *30* hours ago'."

"I know, I got a beep, then I had to pick up the message then I had to drive six hours to the meeting and meet with my boss and drive back. I could have stopped and maybe had a nap but I didn't, did I? And it was more like fifteen hours."

"Well, what happened?"

"The guy who started our department died. It was natural. He was about a hundred years old. But come on, calm down. We've got to talk some things out." Michael walked into the kitchenette. "I thought I left a little coffee maker in here."

"It's under the sink." Tim watched him impatiently. "I'm fucked, aren't I?"

Michael pulled the coffee maker and can of coffee out. "Maybe not, but we need to come up with a better plan than the one my boss gave me."

"What'd he say?"

"She. She said to pay you off and have you disappear. She's even enrolled some people to help with that."

"See? I was worried about that. I knew in the end they would fuck me over."

"Tim. You've got to calm down. Dude, we're in this together." Michael turned around to see Tim holding a gun on him. "Are you high? Put that away."

"Why pay all that money to have me disappear when you can save a few bucks?"

It took all of Michael's strength to stay relaxed. "Dude. They think you're a *fucking* hero. They want to keep you safe, not do away with you." In a calculated sign of trust, Michael turned his back to Tim and flipped on the coffee maker, and then side stepped to the refrigerator, "Any milk?"

"So what's the plan?" Tim demanded.

Michael pointed to a chair next to the rickety drop leaf table. "Can I?"

Tim nodded and tucked his weapon into his waistline of his jeans.

Michael rubbed his face. "Okay," he started, "they want to make it look like you're gone. And then in a little while have you resurface with a new identity."

"But then it looks like I'm guilty—"

"Where'd you even get a gun, man?"

"It was my dad's service revolver. Look, at some point I'm going to have to reconnect the batteries in these phones. I need a story to tell people. I think we should have more of a plan then we do now. We need a plan B and C. At least I put in to take off next week from work - for the divorce and to move my stuff out of the house. That will buy us some time."

"Yeah, but they'll get around to you. First, whoever was in charge of this at Spectorgies will retrace their steps, then they'll pressure The Hayward, then The Hayward will have to retrace all their steps. They'll realize Spectorgies sent you and think you were acting under orders. Which is where I'm hoping it will stall for a little while. The bigger problem is Spectorgies already put out some feelers to possible buyers, which just accelerates everything."

"So if I don't disappear right away then The Hayward will go after Spectorgies, or the other way around?"

"It doesn't matter -- it's the same result. The worst and best thing would be for you just to get fired by Spectorgies. But I doubt they'll do that. It's not like they're going to do is make this public. But the trick right now would be to keep them guessing as to your whereabouts. Then when it goes on the black market and you're still around, completely oblivious to any questioning they put you through, then who will be the wiser?"

"What about getting another message to my NSA handler?"

"Don't. Just throw – better yet, give me that burner and I'll have it shredded. They still might get involved. Coffee?"

Tim nodded.

Michael poured them both a cup and sat back down. "Look, Tim, you are going to need nerves of steel for the next few weeks if we take this route. And y'know, you just pulled a gun on *me.*"

"I pulled a gun on you because I'm sitting on ten million dollars. I'd pull a gun on my *mother* for ten million dollars."

Michael laughed. "Fair enough."

They sat for another moment sipping their coffee.

Finally, Tim spoke calmly. "So basically it's witness protection: lose contact with everyone and everything I know or take my chances and risk what? Possible jail time?"

"No. I don't know if it would go that far."

"But the FBI isn't going to admit anything, would they?"

"No. I can't imagine they would, not for you, not for something on this big of a scale. They want to use the device to lure people out of the woodwork."

"Who?"

"Arms dealers, goats, I don't know. Oh! I almost forgot, God I'm tired. So remember when we talked about your wife's friend, Sally?"

"Yeah, they live across the street now."

"Well, her parents have resurfaced and moved to Ohlone Island. They were old friends of the guy, Elliot, who started our department. My boss said they approached her at the funeral. Guess where they are?"

"I don't know."

"Downstairs."

"What?"

"They opened the Auld Alliance Café down on High Street. My boss said they were experts at disappearing acts back in the day and were going to help in your disappearance."

"What do you mean? I thought they were CIA?"

"Retired."

"So, does Sally know this? I mean, is she working with them?"

"I have no idea."

"So she's a CIA agent here and using the HUD job as a cover?"

"I don't know that for sure. I think the department is working that out now."

"Wow."

"I know, right under our noses. But look, coffee or not, I need sleep. Give me a few hours and we'll finish the plan. I think you should call your wife or ex-wife and make a time for you to come by and get your stuff. But not a real time, we'll just show up unannounced. Where's the Aurora?"

"Are you kidding? I hid it in the 10th hour of your disappearance."

"Here?"

"No. I hid it at our place."

"You left and went back to your house? You took that chance? I told you to stay put."

"You told me you'd be right back. How did I not know you didn't have a bullet in the back of the head or something?"

"So, where is it?"

"I told you it's safe. I hid it at my -- Annie's house."

"Okay. Two hours?" Michael got up and walked toward the front room where he unrolled a sleeping bag and climbed in it."

"Yeah. I'll be playing with the lint bunnies."

Michael did not fall asleep right away. He was very worried about this whole mission. And he was frustrated, because now he had to gain Tim's trust back. He had to teach Tim to suppress the urge to fight or flight somehow. But what if instead of playing cat and mouse and making Tim act innocent they were obvious about it. Let Spectorgies know they had it? What could be the worst-case scenario with that?

CHAPTER 5

STANDARD PRACTICE

During the early part of the 1800's, Ohlone Island was still a marshy farming peninsula attached to Oakland. About halfway through the century, the railroad rolled into town and transformed Ohlone from a farming community into a major transportation hub. The transcontinental terminus was located at the Ohlone Mole where commuters and goods were ferried into San Francisco or put on local trains that would trudge their loads up and down the West Coast.

By 1900, the expanding need for shipping facilities along the western coast led to the dredging of a deep canal through the marshland that connected Ohlone to Oakland. Ohlone Island became home to the best-equipped shipyard in the country at that time. For decades, through World

War I and the Depression, Ohlone Island remained an electric train maintenance and repair facility.

Then for twenty more years after World War II, the southeast edge of Ohlone Island was frantic with freight and manufacturing activity. The estuary shoreline, a stone-skipping toss from the Port of Oakland, ushered manufactured goods brought in from across the country on the railroad and across the estuary onto the freighters.

But now only a few small, local businesses fill the mainly vacant storefronts: a knife forger, a sail fabricator, a custom furniture maker. Most of the rusting tin-sided warehouses that crowd the shoreline stand vacant and derelict. Less than a handful are filled with products awaiting distribution to the mainland. The old train tracks still divide the street.

Annie knew of an old whistle stop depot along these tracks that had been renovated into a small internet café. They advertised an open mic on Tuesday nights, but mainly they were a morning muffin and coffee stop for commuters headed to Oakland via the South Bridge. "I think it's out of the way enough to suit our purposes," Annie explained to Tessa as she parked the car. The first step in Tessa's plan involved a little 'low grade' hacking into emails. So Annie led Tessa in and they sat down at a wooden table. Tessa pulled her laptop out of her bag and set it down.

"I'll get us something to drink," Annie offered.

The Barista, a young female student with black hair pulled into a ponytail and tattoos so thick up her arms that Annie thought they were sleeves, was wearing a poodle skirt. She got up from one of the five tables where she had been reading a thick textbook and stood behind the counter.

"If they have Chamomile.....If not, just a double espresso with a dash of milk."

"Okay." Annie didn't argue.

Sally made herself as flat and as horizontal as possible on the bed and stared at the ceiling. She was furious at Tessa. She would never let it show of course, but that takes some serious chutzpa to make such a careless mistake. To *mail* something so valuable and then just to expect everyone to help her retrieve it. Lorna doesn't need to be protected from the actions of her own past, Sally thought. She needs to be protected from Tessa's debacle.

Sally took deep and measured breaths. Slowly counting as she inhaled, held it, and released. The problem with Tessa is manipulation. She's like a serial manipulator. But the question is when did she become so? Did she manipulate Lorna's parents into adopting her? Of course she did. She was a kid who was going blind in a family who stole her insurance money and left her to fend for herself. Whatever. That's fine, Sally thought, but must she be so duplicitous?

Sally puffed out the air she had been holding in and focused her thoughts. One thought at a time. She did feel a little ambushed this morning at the airport with Tessa but that's over. If Tessa tries to do some kind of manipulation -- wait a second. Sally sat up in bed. Had Tessa ambushed her at the airport because she already knew this package had been stolen? How long had Tessa been sitting on Sally's information? Tessa made it sound as if she was doing Sally a favor. She rolled over onto her side and placed Lorna's pillow over her head. She was the only person who could influence Lorna not to get involved in this – Sally followed the logical sequence. Leaving her with only one question. What is she going to do about it?

After ordering, Annie sat back down and looked at Tessa's laptop. She was surprised to see it was just an ordinary personal computer. "She gave me the code to log on to their network," Annie said pulling the computer in front of her.

"I pulled off the screen reader software so you can use it," Tessa said as she sat back from the computer, nudging it away. "How much do you know about hacking?"

"Just enough to get myself in trouble," rolling her eyes to no effect.

"Excellent," Tessa smiled.

"We're going to have to do this quick. It'll still register that they had an intruder but with any luck we won't go through the main frame and just hack into the emails of your, um...." Annie looked around at the Barista as another customer came in.

"Right," Tessa agreed.

"Generally, most smaller companies don't check these logs on the weekends."

"Let's hope they don't. David said he would be at Lorna and Sally's about four o'clock."

Annie was typing and talking at the same time. "Oh, we'll be done long before then. It'll give us time to read the emails. What are we looking for by the way?"

"Anything that gives him away."

Annie stopped typing. "But would that be on his company's email? Is he that stupid?"

"No, but we're looking for plans, orders, anything involving a new product rollout."

"You wouldn't happen to know if Glen's got a hotmail, yahoo, or a g-mail account as well?"

"I'm sure he does."

"Good, I can check those too," Annie offered cheerfully.

Tessa sat back. "Oh you are naughty. I like that."

The barista came over with their drinks, sat them down, and smiled pitifully at Tessa, which made Annie chuckle.

"Thank you," Annie said, putting Tessa's tea in front of her. "The honey and sugar are on your left."

"Thanks." Tessa turned her face toward the warmth of the sun. "I won't look. I don't want to be a witness to your criminal activities."

After a few minutes Annie asked, "So, how far do we want to go back in the business emails?"

"Can we do a search for terms and decide that way?"

"No," Annie replied. "We need to get in and out of this."

"Okay, three months' worth?"

"That's fine," Annie said.

And with a few more clicks on the laptop, the deed was done. Tessa kept her voice low. "We need to talk about how to handle David too."

"What do you mean?" Annie asked.

"I just think it's very important to keep him close by. Do you mind being a honey trap?"

"Well, yes, but no. How much honey?

"Just a drop, a whiff."

"Oh, yeah. That's okay. I just can't get to involved, you know."

"No, of course not. No, I don't mean have sex with the guy. I don't know….I'm not really too sure about him and I'm just trying to remember exactly who I told about my change of flight."

"I didn't even know you were coming in town," Annie said.

"Well, Lorna has had a lot on her plate recently. You know it probably kept slipping her mind until the last minute. You know how she can get sometimes."

Annie was a little taken aback at this but said nothing.

"My sister likes to stay busy and, sometimes, I think she just overwhelms herself. It's not that she becomes unreliable but she can spread herself a bit thin is all. Mind you, I'd trust her above anyone else in the world. As long as she stays focused on the task at hand she's like a hawk circling around its prey."

"That's a good way to put it." Annie found this to be very true about her friend. "She does like the chaos but then she can be very focused when she needs to be."

"How about those emails?" Tessa asked. "I'm afraid you'll have to read them to me."

"What did you want to say about David?" Annie asked.

"Let's get to those emails first before I jump to any conclusions about David."

Annie tapped the computer back to life. "Okay, so I can do that word search now and I'm going to put in Landsea, rollout, and then – whoa." Annie stopped typing. "There are like 40 emails with Landsea in them." Annie paused as she skimmed through the emails. "They are having a meeting with Colby next Thursday."

"Oh that's just *great* then," Tessa sighed. "Do they have an agenda?"

"Boy, do they!" Annie exclaimed.

David Poole walked his bike the last hundred yards to the corner of Saint Charles Place. A few more projects like this one and he might be able to get out of this rat race and strike out on his own. David casually glanced up at the house numbers. When he saw a shade move, he pulled his bike helmet down further. Tessa had been so obsequious about this meeting. But women are like that, especially when they want something from you or when they are negotiating. Monday was supposed to be their first and, as far as he knew, only meeting. Maybe she was just happy with his product and actually wanted to thank him casually. He checked his watch as he walked up the few steps onto the porch and parked his bike next to the railing. It was three thirty, a little early, but he liked employing the element of surprise.

"David?" The front door opened to a tall blonde woman whom he didn't recognize.

"Hi. Is it okay if I leave my bike on the porch?"

"Oh sure, it'll be fine there. Come on in." Lorna held the door open wider. "I'm Lorna, Tessa's sister. She's out on an errand but she'll be back in a few minutes."

"I'm sorry, I'm so early."

"It's no worry. Come in and have a seat."

Annie was deeply touched at how understanding Tessa could be. It was comforting to hear Tessa talk about her own stories of love and loss from the distance that only time and a keen self-awareness can bring. It was giving Annie a lot to think about besides being alone and miserable with the self-pity she had been feeling.

"I think a deeper question to ask yourself is not why, but why now?" Tessa asked.

"I blame his job," Annie admitted.

"What about that?"

"The travel, the stress, and I guess the whole change in him all of that brought on."

"But it's strange that he's just handing over everything the two of you built. The house, the pets – and a lot of the money?"

"Yeah. It's like he was doing me a favor."

"By leaving?"

"Before, I was just blinded by the words, 'let's get a divorce'. He said it as if we were planning a vacation. And the next thing I know, he's looking online for information on how to do it."

"He said that like he had found a solution, you mean?"

"Now that I think about it, yes."

This struck Tessa. When Spectorgies bought out Tim's former employer, it was a forgone conclusion that Tim would be out the door with the rest of the teams and replaced by Spectorgies people.

Tim, deeply worried about the lack of prospects in the job market, had mentioned his impending unemployment to Lorna. Lorna told Tessa, and Tessa quietly pulled some strings with her contacts in the NSA, who holds the majority of Spectorgies contracts. Tim's human resource team made the transition successfully, so the news of this divorce and hearing about Tim's radical behavior change worried Tessa. Had her contacts with the NSA influenced Spectorgies to keep Tim on so they could use him as an inside man?

Annie watched as Tessa put her hand out toward her. "Listen," Tessa's usual booming voice dropped to a near whisper. "I'm so glad you've found time to spend with us during this. It's the hardest thing to do but it's so important you keep moving forward, one shaky step after another. Everything changes, love changes, we go through changes, phases, so we can keep growing. Sometimes we have to change ourselves so we can give to the relationships we have or want to have. It doesn't sound like there is any hate or anything untoward in Tim's heart. I can't answer to that but the best thing you can do right now is to be true to yourself. And make a plan for yourself."

Annie took a deep breath and blinked back the tears that had welled up in her eyes. "I know you're right. But it's hard."

"Yes. What time is it?"

"Oh gosh, it's 3:30. We should be getting back."

Despite the pep talk she gave Annie, Tessa could not shake the ominous feeling she had about this divorce. Something was definitely wrong with this divorce. Maybe she would talk to Sally about it after this other mess gets cleaned up.

Lorna had been learning all about the mini- marathons and various triathlons in which David had participated over the last couple of years when Sally came back downstairs.

"Oh, hi," she said to David and Lorna.

"Hi honey, this is David. He's Tessa's audio guy in this last um, thing. David, this is my partner, Sally."

"It's nice to meet you," Sally said.

"Yes," David said.

Lorna smiled at Sally. "How was your nap?"

"I don't know. I was asleep," Sally said, smiling back.

"There's coffee in the kitchen," Lorna said and sat back down with David. If Tessa and Annie didn't get back soon, she was going to have to listen to more about David's heroic and athletic prowess. But just then the front door opened.

"Don't you lock the doors around here? You don't know what scum – oh David, are you here?" Tessa stood in the doorway and bellowed.

Lorna laughed out, more for David's than for humor's sake.

David laughed along. "You *must* be Tessa."

Tessa walked purposefully into the room and stood with her hand out. David took his cue and moved in front of her, taking her hand in his.

"We were just—" Lorna began.

"Come in have a seat," David jumped in, playing host.

Lorna played along and played servant to his new host role. "David, let me get you some more water. Tessa? Coffee?"

"Please, thank you," Tessa answered and sat down.

"I'll help," Annie offered and scurried away with Lorna to the kitchen.

Sally met them coming out of the kitchen and was herded back in.

"Am I invisible?" Annie asked.

Lorna was fuming. "I'm sorry but that was weird. I don't like this guy. I mean, I *really* don't like this guy. Arrogant mother-...."

"Why? Should we get word to Tessa? I mean, we're pretty sure it was Sibley but there was no obvious or definite answers," Annie suggested.

"What did you find?" Lorna asked Annie.

"Plenty. Glenn Colby is nasty! He was sex- bragging in a couple of emails..."

"What a dumb ass," Sally interjected. "When are people going to learn?"

"What's the plan?" Lorna asked Annie.

"Tessa's going to put David through the paces and then she's going to let him in on what's happened. He may run out screaming or he may just have to be coerced a little, she said. What's he like?"

"He's arrogant, to the point of rude. I don't know. This could be a slow motion train crash. We better get back in there."

When Annie handed David his water, he stood up. "I'm so sorry. I didn't see you come in. I'm David Poole."

"It's okay, I'm Annie, Lorna's neighbor," Annie answered.

There was no mistaking that David was bowled over by Annie. His body language went from a humble posture, shoulders down, chest in, and lowered eyes up to a full-blown Bannie Rooster strut in one breath.

Lorna recognized it first. "Tessa, I'm sorry to interrupt but can I steal you for two seconds? A couple of things came in while you were gone so I just need you for a minute..."

Tessa stood up, grabbing her purse. "David, let me just take a minute so I can—"

"It's no problem," David answered, smiling wide.

Lorna led Tessa down the hall to her office and shut the door.

"What does he look like?" Tessa asked, turning around.

"Five-ten, maybe five-eleven. Dark hair, green eyes, round face, straight teeth, soft jaw-line….he wears contacts. And he's arrogant, in love with Annie, and rode a bike to a business meeting."

"Well, they do that here." Tessa pulled out her little remote from her purse and pressed the button. The house emitted a low hum. "Do you think he'll notice?"

"Yes, Tessa!" Lorna hissed. "And I don't know if you can trust him entirely. Seriously, if you let him in on this, you may be opening the door to bad things. What about the emails?"

"I couldn't tell if Glen was super savvy or a complete idiot. But there was nothing that indicated a new product or a side deal. He's got a couple of meetings next week with Landsea about navigational equipment. He could also just be using navigational equipment as a code word. I'm going to have to take the chance with David. We're going to need him. Just follow my lead, take note of his body language. We'll see," Tessa said and opened the door back up.

"I would love to stop in there sometime…" David was saying to Annie when they returned. Sally sat relatively invisible in an armchair grinning at Fortitude, who was sitting on her lap.

Tessa eased into the other armchair. "I'm sorry. So, David."

"Yes, Tessa." David smiled. He actually didn't seem to notice the low hum that radiated around them.

"I wanted to bring you over today, initially, to thank you personally and spend some time together before Monday when I make my presentation to the clients."

David squared himself to her now. "Right."

"As you know, when we make certain products we don't always let the individual component makers know exactly what their components are designed for, or we lie about it."

David nodded. "Standard practice."

"This wasn't an audio interface for the blind to download GPS maps or for sailing equipment. That was my cover story because it is for Landsea Corp. You actually built the audio interface portion of a handheld device that works a bit like a torrent, relaying on open and closed networks with any RF, LAN, or Wi-Fi signals available."

David laughed. "They are completely different signal generators," he shrugged. "It's impossible."

"It does it with the DAC and a vector signal receiver."

David's robust expression fell. "JTRS?" he asked, referring to the proprietary methods the military often creates for their own custom waveforms in their communication systems.

"It's powerful. And virtually untraceable."

Annie, Sally, and Lorna were completely lost in this conversation of acronyms. But they could read the seriousness in David's expressions.

"What," David started, appearing pale, "may I ask, is its application?"

"It's essentially just a hard drive, like any handheld computer, but it doesn't need capacity as it is designed to simply move data from one server to another server."

The entire explanation fell on Annie. "Ho-ly crap," she mumbled.

Lorna looked at their faces. "David, would you like a little bourbon with your water?"

"I would, thank you." David seemed to be humbled again.

Lorna got up and left the room. She needed air. Tessa had sucked all the wind out of the living room. When she came back in with the bourbon, she heard Sally saying something about satellite pinpointing. And Annie mumbling, 'Ho-ly crap' again. Now Lorna was feeling genuinely sorry for the guy. Wait until Tessa tells him it was stolen, she thought.

"David," Tessa began. "I'm curious. Did you have any conversations with anyone about this project?"

"No," David answered a little too quickly.

"No one you could have mentioned it to, at all?"

"Well, I don't know, maybe a couple of people. Why?"

"Who?"

"I don't know, people. Friends mainly."

"What did you tell them?"

"That I was working on an audio interface for TollComm. And that your request about the low capacity was odd."

"Anyone from Sibley Systems?"

"Where is this going?"

"I'm just curious. We've hit a snag."

"I don't like this. Why did you bring up Sibley?" David scoffed. "What possible snag could you have hit working on a device like this? Oh, I don't know, maybe you've broken every possible law in the FCC? No. I don't want to hear anymore. My contract specifically outlined what my portion was in this. It's my best defense," David said, standing up.

"No, you've got it wrong. I haven't broken *any* laws and I certainly don't go in with the likes of Sibley Systems. *That much* I can assure you."

"David, I'm just as shocked as you are," Annie chimed in, reaching up and touching David's arm. "Please, let's just hear her out."

Lorna watched Annie - *Wow, she's good.* David sat back down.

David rubbed an eyebrow. "So, what's the snag?"

"I have every reason to believe that Glenn Colby intercepted a package that contained the device."

"You *mailed* it?"

Tessa countered his incredulity. "You think they'd let me on a plane with that?"

David leaned over and put his head in his hands. "Glenn Colby...is evil."

Annie took her cue. "Well, we just have to get it back."

"Do you remember that big technology security consortium a while back? Glenn and Sibley were in charge of coordinating all the players," David said, defeated.

"No. Don't give up yet, David. I shipped the package overnight, the day before yesterday. My meeting with Landsea isn't until Monday. I wasn't even supposed to be here until Sunday. I changed my flight a day ahead so I could be here when the package arrived. So it is very possible they are unaware that I even know it's missing right now."

David shook his head.

"It is a window of opportunity, a small one, but still…." Lorna prodded.

Sally cut in. "What are you saying? How would we even look for it?"

"Not you, Maestro," Tessa turned on Sally. "The rest of us would get a slap on the wrist and I could cover it for us. You however, work for Uncle Sam. And there would be no cover I could possible throw for you. You'd be disbarred and whatever other God-awful things would await you."

Sally cut her eyes to David. He sat goggle-eyed and said, "Why don't you just call the police?"

Tessa smiled. "Because they don't deal in corporate espionage."

Annie piped up. She needed to keep things moving before David split on them. "So, what's the plan?"

"You'll help?" Tessa asked her.

"Sure, and I have a friend who worked for Sibley for a while. I'm sure I can get him to help." Maybe David would see this as a networking possibility.

"I don't want this to get out, Annie. I think less is more here." Tessa turned her head toward Lorna.

"I'm your sister. Just tell me what to do."

David sat weighing his options as Tessa continued. "Someone as arrogant as Glenn Colby is not going to put too many miles between himself and his new prize. I happen to know that he has a boat at Ohlone Yacht Club he stays on sometimes during the weekend."

"That's like walking distance to their little campus in the corporate park," Lorna added.

"So the first two places we can look will be the Sibley offices and the boat. Now, I pulled the memory chip from it before I sent it, so it's not likely he's going to be playing with it over on his boat," Tessa said, revealing her plan.

"You think it's over in their offices? Just sitting there?" Sally asked.

"I think that's the first place I'd look. Aren't those buildings all laid out the same?" Lorna said.

David finally spoke up. "Yeah, they are."

"Good, so we've got a time and place."

"When? I mean, wouldn't they work all hours? Especially with a new toy like this?" Lorna asked.

"No, they're probably testing it in their little lab now. Come Saturday, they'll put it up and celebrate their coup," Tessa answered.

"Look Tessa, I just really appreciate the opportunity you gave me to work with you but I think I should go. I don't want to be rude or ungrateful but this is a little over my head."

"Well, David, thank you." Tessa stood and put her hand out. "I think you did a great job and I'm the one who is grateful, you have a bright future ahead of you. Good luck."

David shook it, and Annie noticed that he was looking somewhat rejected.

Annie walked David to the front porch. "So, how about dinner at the Auld Alliance Café?"

David put his bike helmet on. "I can't, I made plans for tonight. How about brunch tomorrow though?"

"Sounds great. Around eleven?"

"See you there," David said and walked his bike down the stairs.

Lorna picked up the glasses and returned them to the kitchen. Sally remained in the armchair as Patience leapt into Tessa's lap. Tessa had successfully placed Sally in one corner, silenced by her past indiscretion.

"It must be frustrating for you," Sally said softly.

"More than you can possibly imagine," Tessa responded while stroking Patience.

CHAPTER 6

GREED AND LOATHING

The San Francisco Ferry Building houses a densely packed matrix of overpriced gourmet and housewares shops. There, those possessing the most discriminating of tastes may purchase, for forty dollars a pound, lavender honey, the sweet glucose alternative made from the regurgitation of slavish insects. And while nobody balks at the unseemly prices, it will be only a few weeks before, as a matter of course, a group will board a bus to go somewhere else and *boycott* the honey in order to bring attention to the plight of the humble and extorted honey bee. All the same, the Ferry Building, with its well-manicured, finely tuned image, is still a significant weekend destination well trodden by locals and tourists alike.

Brian Hodge took his time picking out proper olive oil. Truth be told, he knew very little about any oil. But as he was, in fact, moving up in the world, this information could be useful for him. What he did not understand, if he was being honest, is why is all this shit so expensive? When did simply knowing that you shouldn't eat food grown in plastic and recycled adult diapers make you a food expert or justify charging these astronomical prices for bee puke? And this is the twenty first century; the cotton gin was invented in the eighteenth century. Why should he have to pay extra money because some asshole refused to learn to produce food efficiently and then advertised his stubborn product as "painstakingly hand made or hand grown" shit. Brian glanced at the price tag on a bottle of honey. He stared at the bottle doing a quick equation in his mind. Even at the rate of inflation from 1985 to the present, honey should not cost forty dollars a bottle.

A bead of sweat ran down his back, and stuck his shirt to his back. An appreciation for the better things had not brought him here to buy lovingly nurtured vegetables picked at the brink of ripeness or the local bee's honey. The true source of his agitation came from Joshua N. Edwards himself. Why meet here at the pretend food expert's Mecca? This is not where big deals were made. They should be meeting on a golf course or at one of their labs. The more he thought about selling the Aurora copy behind the back of the NSA, the less comfortable in his skin he felt. How do guys like Edwards do this? The money he had made from the sale was extraordinary, but right now, he'd give it all back for a decent night's sleep. Brian was suddenly aware of a man standing in his sightline and he looked up.

"My name is Morey." The balding man was dressed in a tattered running suit.

"Good." Brian was worried he had stumbled into one of those weekend sex pickups.

"The ferry leaves in a few minutes. Here's your ticket. Don't miss it." Morey handed Brian the ticket and walked away.

Brian made his way out to the pier and thought, maybe something went wrong with the Aurora in the simulator. That would be good, because then he could give the money back and call it a day.

Once he got on the boat he saw Joshua Edwards sitting on the back deck of the ferry. He saw Morey too, sitting inside the cabin reading a paper. He walked out to the back deck. Edwards shook his head no at Brian, then took out his cell phone out and made a show of taking out the battery. Brian felt the stinging sensation that something was very wrong here. Brian followed Edwards' actions and took the battery out of his cell phone before sitting down.

"This last trip you made down to Earthsat in San Diego," Edwards began, "was it with the same team who built the hardware for the device?"

"Yes," Brian answered.

"Did you have the *our* device with you at that time?"

"No."

"So, then when we met with the NSA, you had no idea what you were delivering to me in your case?"

"I delivered the software to you."

"No. You didn't. Are you sure you delivered the correct software to the NSA?"

"Yes. I was there when they tested it at Earthsat."

"You have a problem then."

"I do?"

Edwards nodded. "But don't worry. I've got it covered for you. The Hayward is going to work on cyber assets for Spectorgies. I've got a guy waiting with the paperwork for you to sign."

Brian shook his head without understanding. "What are you saying?"

"The Aurora doesn't work. So either someone at the NSA was on to your duplicitous nature and switched out your copy or you duped me. But I don't think you're that stupid."

Brian stared out at the choppy water in the bay.

Edwards smiled awkwardly. "No, I didn't think you were. But I figure you have enough in contracts over there to cover what I paid for the Aurora. So, we're good. You'll stay on, of course, draw a paycheck, but we'll handle your day-to-day operations and any further contracts coming in for you. You are a clever programmer and I want to help you out."

Brian was aghast. What the hell was he talking about? Spectorgies is taking over his company? "Wait a minute. Just hold on. You're saying the Aurora malfunctioned so you think you're going to take over my company? I'm not signing anything. I'll happily refund your money and we can call it a day."

Edwards laughed. "You don't *refund* ten million dollars." He patted Brian on the shoulders. "The man that is waiting for you at the Ohlone Pier is going to ask you a series of questions about who worked on the Aurora, who was at The Hayward while you were constructing the copy, and who else knew you were making this sale. And then you are going to sign the papers. It's your only way out, Brian. Let me at least do that for you."

"I'm not signing anything. I'm going to retain legal counsel and then I might turn myself in to the NSA. But my company is not for sale or up for a take-over bid. You aren't that stupid either, I'm sure," Brian challenged Edwards.

Edwards nodded and switched tactics. "Fair enough. That's your choice of course. I'm just trying to help you out here. But you'll at least answer my investigator's questions at the pier?"

"Yeah sure. And you'll at least give me a chance to look at the Aurora copy and check out the software for yours," Brian said, backing down.

"Sure, sure. He has it with him, I think. You guys can drop it off at The Hayward. You play Pac-Man?" Edwards asked.

Brian shrugged. "Of course."

Edwards got up from his seat. "Then that will be a big help for you," he said, and walked inside the ferryboat cabin.

Center Street, which conveniently runs down the middle of Ohlone, has wide bike lanes along the roadway. Palm trees and Coastal Oaks reaching tall and straight into the sky pepper the street with their long shadows. Annie took a deep breath of the fragrant air filled with lavender, honeysuckle, and salty sea grasses as she rolled her bike to a stop at the light.

Perhaps Tessa was right and it was time for a life change. The light turned green and Annie continued on, lost in her thoughts. She could find a new job, maybe even start her own business doing consulting work; she knows a lot of people. Last year she did that online marketing for the winery by herself and she does know a lot of business owners. She would have to work on a client base. Focus, Annie! she told herself as she parked her bike next to David's on the sidewalk bike rack and wrapped her chain to her helmet and front tire.

The new Auld Alliance Café was bumping with an eager clientele. The door had been propped open, letting the sweet air mingle with the smell of fresh baked bread. The front door was filled with shoppers and diners. On the left wall, people crowded along the service counter peering down and pointing at the glass case. Others mingled along the right side shelves that held delicacies from "across the pond." Annie smiled approvingly. What a great addition to the island's shopping district. She made her way past the crowd, through a small hallway, and out into a covered garden. The dozen or so tables were filled with customers who ate hungrily or chatted with one another over steaming cups. David sat amongst them giving Annie a little wave when he caught her eye.

"I thought it was best to grab a table first," he said as she sat down with him.

"My gosh, what a grand opening though!" Annie said cheerfully. "It doesn't look like they have table service. Let me go order for us. What would you like?"

"I'll get it." David stood up.

"No, you guard the fort. I'll hunt and gather."

David smiled. "Coffee and like a croissant?"

"Do you like sweet or savory?"

"Savory."

Annie nodded and returned to the service counter and stood in line enjoying the atmosphere. She could start marketing for small businesses like this one. She looked behind the counter for the people who looked like they might be the owners. Several people scurried about putting together crepes, omelets, sandwiches and drinks. Two young Hispanic men cooked while a young woman took charge of the glass case, and an elderly Asian woman rang people up at the register. There was a rhythm to it all that matched the French jazz music playing lightly under the chattering voices and dish clatter. Intermittently, a tall but stooped elderly white man with a thinning comb over and a large nose came out from the swinging doors to bring in fresh baked goods or to take away an overflowing dishpan. This time he shuffled out and over to the Asian woman and whispered something to her. She nodded and went about her duties. Annie made a mental note - they must be the owners.

Sally and Roberta discussed wardrobe strategy as they walked through the streets of San Francisco's Hayes Valley district. Sally was just happy to get out of the house and leave behind her frustrations and suspicions for a little while.

"I'm thinking three suits. Blue, grey, brown, or maybe black – neutral colors. And I'll just rotate them," Roberta was saying.

"That's what I do," Sally explained. "I've got one very good suit, the one I use if I have to be in court or something, and the rest are dailies. But I keep several shirts and sweaters to interchange with them. We can just go anyplace to get those. In your line of work you will probably go through them quickly. But the suits you can keep for a couple of years."

"Okay. Yeah, I should do that. But maybe I'll get a couple to wear when I have to make court appearances. Then a couple more for daily wear."

"You need to make sure the court suits are lined," Sally added.

Roberta looked inside the glass window of the store. "This is going to get expensive."

Sally nodded and opened the door to the boutique. "If you want to look good it is."

When it was her turn to order Annie raised her voice over the din. "Two ham and gouda croissants and two medium coffees, for here."

Annie continued sideling toward the cashier, ducking and bobbing so people just coming in could look into the glass case.

"What did you order?" the Asian lady asked her when she arrived at the checkout counter.

"Two ham and gouda croissants and two medium coffees, for here," Annie repeated.

"Eight-fifty."

"Oh, but it should be more. I had the coffees," Annie said.

"No, it's our grand opening this weekend. Free coffee with your meals."

"Thank you." Annie handed the woman her money. "That's very clever. I really think you guys are going to be a hit."

The Asian woman smiled. Her eyes twinkled up at Annie. "I hope so."

When she got back to the table, David was reading a piece of the newspaper and folded it up when she sat down.

"Thank you. Are they still crazy busy up there?" he asked.

"Yeah, I can't imagine what it must have been like for the breakfast rush. It's already almost eleven thirty."

David took a big bite of his sandwich. "Oh. Mmm. Oh my God."

Annie smiled and daintily cut hers in half before taking a bite. They both chewed in silence for a few moments.

Finally David asked, "Are you still going through with it?"

Annie nodded, still chewing.

David wiped his mouth and cleared his throat. "Listen, we don't really know each other yet but I would be remiss if I didn't share my, uh, misgivings about the situation. Okay?"

Annie nodded, only half listening. This is *really* a good croissant.

David continued, "Ya' know, people like Tessa. These powerful and rich people, it's fine for them to go on playing their games but for you and I – if we get caught, we go to jail. You think they're going to dirty their hands helping us out? It's fine for her sister and that other one, whatever, women like that stick together."

Annie paused in her chewing. Who's *women like that?* Did he just call Sally, *that other one?* So casually, so dismissive. Now she knew why Lorna didn't like him. "How do you know this?" she asked, feigning interest.

"I've seen it happen with Glenn Colby. Paul, a friend of mine used to work for him. Glenn used to pass off Paul's stuff as his own. You know that consortium I was talking about? Paul put that whole thing together through his contacts. He put together the goals, the players, and the agreements. That was all Paul. Then this asshole Colby waltzes in off the golf course at the last minute taking all the credit, making new friends and alliances, boosting himself into the higher echelons of the technology ruling class. It was disgusting."

"Oh, well I'm sorry for your friend. But, this is really apples and oranges you're talking about. Tessa doesn't work in these networks or old boy clubs. How could she? And she always hires the same people over and over. No, I'll take my chances with Tessa. She could just as easily hire a couple of mercenaries to go in there and smash the whole place up, grab her stuff, and burn Colby to the ground. But she's not. She's going to go in quietly and take back her work, and yours too, I might add. I think that says a lot about her." Satisfied with herself, Annie took the last bite of her sandwich.

"But, what I'm saying is she's not actually doing it. She's getting people to do it for her, expendable people."

"Well, what do you care? You already walked out on her. Your hands aren't dirty here."

"I didn't walk out on her -- I wasn't given much of a choice. She's like, 'Hey I want you guys to break the law against a very powerful person. Who's in?'"

Annie laughed. "Yeah, that's Tessa. But I'm in. I completely trust her."

"You must."

"So your friend Paul isn't the only victim of Colby's you know. Now you are too."

"No, Tessa is. My job was done and done quite well."

"And I bet you were paid well too," Annie added knowingly.

David paused and stared at Annie for a moment.

"I'm just saying, David. Look, we all hear gossip about who's a stinker to work for and who screws over who. And in all of the blogs and all of the magazine articles, have you ever once heard or read anything derogatory about Tessa or TollComm?"

"No."

"No. Expendable or not, I would rather share an experience – good or bad - with someone with that kind of reputation than to be seen sitting by and doing nothing."

David sat back, scratched his ear, and took a sip of coffee. "I see that."

"And I'm quite sure, if Tessa had her sight, that she would be doing this herself. I don't care how bold and clever she acts, you know some part of her must absolutely hate this. Would this have even happened if she were sighted? It's disgusting is what it is. Hell, I'm happy to participate. Maybe I'll burn his shit down." The word, shit, came out of Annie's mouth like a foreign tongue. But she liked the bravado using the word 'shit' gave her.

David sat quietly nodding to himself. "I came here to convince you to back out of this," he said, continuing to nod. "And now I'm in. Man, I didn't come off as too big of a dick, did I?"

"No, not at all. And I didn't really come here to convince you otherwise. I'm sure you have your reasons and Tessa respected that," Annie said, sipping her coffee.

"No, you're right. I guess I just needed to talk it out."

"Well, I'm sure Tessa will be glad to hear of it. But we should stop by the house when we leave here and let her know. I know she's working everything out right now. Did you have plans today or tonight?"

"No – well, speaking of the devil...." David was looking at the doorway behind Annie.

Annie turned around to see Lorna being shown around the covered garden by the elderly cashier. Annie waved at Lorna.

Lorna said something to the cashier, extricated her arm from the lady's grasp, and came over to their table.

"Hi again," she said to David but quickly turned to Annie. "Your cell phone is off."

"Oh no. I'm so sorry." Annie scrambled for her phone.

"I'm just running a couple of errands and Tessa asked me to stop at your place to tell you the meeting time. She wants us all to eat together and go over everything starting around eight o'clock tonight."

"That's so, 'Godfather', of her," David laughed.

Lorna smiled and forced a chuckle. She really, *really* did not like this guy.

"David said he wants back in." Annie blinked innocently up at Lorna.

"Oh that's *great*. David, thank you. Tessa is going to be really happy about this."

"Well, we don't want to upset Tessa." David smiled at Lorna.

Lorna held her tongue. Seriously, this guy can absolutely piss off for all she cared. She regretted making Annie be the honey trap for David.

Annie quickly changed the subject. "By the way, how awesome is this place?"

"Yeah!" Lorna smiled. It's so gonna be our new hangout."

"Nah-uh!" David overacted the part by reaching across and touching Annie's hand. "*It's ours.*"

Lorna's head cocked forward then her face contorted. Her bottom jaw pulled back and her mouth spread the width of her face, baring her teeth. For the first time, Annie witnessed what literally looked like Lorna swallowing her tongue.

"Right on," Lorna finally spat out. "See you guys tonight," she finished, turning and leaving abruptly.

Karen Bernard took her time getting to know Ohlone Island today. She was in no rush. It was beautiful here, kind of a throw back to a bygone era. Or really a throw back to several bygone eras, she thought as she drove around. Starting at the north end of the island, she meandered through the old military base built in the 1940's. Then she took a west side road lined on one side with palm trees that hugged the shoreline beach and parks, and on the other side filled with the ranch houses from the 1970's. She passed back over to the east side though the downtown area on High Street with mostly locally owned shops; bakers, restaurants, a bike shop, a book store, clothing and shoe stores...a butcher. They have a butcher here?

Karen stopped her car. I've fallen into a time warp, she thought. No wonder Sally moved here. At the end of High Street she turned northward again near the east side shoreline and passed through a derelict area filled with rotting warehouses. She noted the boarded up storefronts. That would be a perfect place to hole up for a bit, she thought. She turned again and headed toward the center of town where the magnificent Victorian homes stood their ground defiantly bending time back to the early 19th century. Karen let out a low whistle and checked the address again. Saint Charles Place.

"Let's just do a drive by and see how well Ms. Soucek has done for herself," Karen wondered aloud.

The swift ride back to her house helped cool off Lorna's temper. Her father had once said, 'We need to accept the good and bad in people, especially our friends.' But really, this guy is absolutely irredeemable. Petulant turd, she thought peddling harder. She mocked him aloud, " *'Nah-uh, it's our hangout.'*" Blagh! He's so skeevy!" She rounded onto Saint Charles Place on the wrong side of the street and careened violently. She narrowly missed smacking into a car.

Roberta slammed on the brakes and rolled down her window. "Girl! What is the matter with you?!"

"I'm sorry Roberta. I was driving mad."

"You're driving me mad! Where's your helmet!" Roberta screamed. It wasn't a question.

Lorna put her hand on her head. "Oh! I forgot my helmet."

Roberta pursed her lips. "Mm hmm, yeah!"

"I'm sorry," Lorna said honestly. "You know me. I don't always forget. How was the shopping?"

"Shut up."

Lorna grinned. "You're a good friend, Roberta."

"You better not forget that helmet again Lorna. I'm serious. Give me a heart attack...." Roberta rolled her window back up mumbling as Lorna walked her bike the rest of the way to the front porch.

Lorna walked in to the quiet house and looked around. She listened for a moment. Nothing. She thought briefly about backing out the front door when she heard muffled voices. She walked down the hall to her office. The door was shut but the soft voices were coming from behind the door. She turned the knob and slowly inched the door open. Sally was sitting at her desk soldering something together and Tessa was sitting in the reading chair with Patience perched on her lap.

"How'd it go?" Tessa asked.

"Great. He's in. What are you doing?"

"I'm saudderin'!" Sally said with a laugh.

"We're building an encryption breaker," Tessa explained.

"What's that?"

"It's going to get you into the doors that have code boxes on them. I'll show you how it works when we're done. Sally would have made a great spy."

Lorna laughed. And Sally joined in almost belatedly.

"Yeah," Sally bristled. "I missed my calling."

"Okay. Well, I'm going to take a nap," Lorna said in the lull.

"You just got up," Tessa admonished her.

"So?! I have a really long night ahead and I have to deal with that creepy friend of *yours*. Oh, and by the way, if you're trying to think of a way in which you might express your gratitude to Annie for her help in this....?"

"Go on," Tessa said.

"A trip to Paris might be in order."

Tessa laughed. "If we pull this off, we might all get to go to Paris."

"I'm serious."

"So am I!"

Roberta drove down Center Street and turned left onto High. Lenore's Ladies had a couple of sweaters hanging in the store window which she wanted to try on. But that was it -- no more shopping. She had already spent twice as much as she thought she would today –

"Holy shit!" Roberta made a quick right onto a side street and double-parked the car. She knew that Asian guy. What was his name? That's the guy Detective Keeling pulled out of the estuary the night of that boat blast. That's right! He was an FBI agent, or said he was. What the hell is he doing here again? She watched him walk down the side street and let himself in to the side door of the Lemon Sud.

She sat in her car and put the hazards on. She should let this go. She had promised her daughter that they would do something together today. And he was probably just one of Keeling's nut job informants. She let herself out of the car. No, she thought again, it was Keeling who said he had helped the FBI. Maybe he didn't know about Keeling's new job, she thought. She'll let him know and then head straight back to Lenore's. Roberta slowly opened the outer door and looked up the stairway that led to a second floor above the Lemon Sud. Now why is the FBI holed up in this dump? Roberta had an ominous feeling as she made her way up the creaking stairs.

CHAPTER 7

3 BLIND MICE

Sally cleared away most of the dishes from the table as David, Annie, Lorna, and Tessa talked through the plan again. Tessa kept interjecting 'what if' scenario's to them. What if someone comes in the building when you are going into the offices? What if an alarm is set off? David has seen too many movies, Sally thought. David's answers usually included rescuing 'the girls' or smashing something. Finally Sally sat back down and interjected, "Listen, first and foremost, do not get caught. If anything happens; if someone shows up, someone is already there, an alarm rings, you see buttons on an alarm panel go wonky but there is no sound – that's a silent alarm – get out. And don't stop until you reach our front door. Don't worry about each other, just go."

Tessa nodded. "Yes. Definitely scatter."

Sally continued, "David, how do you know these buildings are the same?"

"I had a friend who worked for Colby. I had gone into their offices once. But our office is in the same office park and has the same layout."

"Where is your friend Paul now?" Annie asked.

"He got a job in Oakland, video game software." David answered.

"Well, I'm glad he got out okay after what Colby put him through."

Lorna leaned her chair back, reached over to the counter, grabbed the encryption breaker, and placed it on the kitchen table in front of them. "Okay you guys, let's not pull another Watergate. Let's go over this again."

"I don't get that reference." Annie looked at Tessa.

Sally explained. "The burglars at Watergate got caught because of the magnetic doors or something like that. The point is to be wary of the security guards."

"I didn't know that." Annie said.

"And don't prop open doors that are supposed to stay shut." Lorna added.

"I wish we could test this somehow." David held up the encryption breaker.

"I did." Tessa said. "But you know what to do if they're using the card keys?"

"Pop the box and hook it up inside." David stretched his arm across the back of Annie's chair.

"Yes, the trick will be to put it back like it never happened." Tessa tapped the table impatiently. "Not that it will buy us more time. But if they really aren't looking for it until Monday, then we don't want to tip them off any earlier."

Lorna rubbed her ears. "That humming is annoying me. I think it's making me sea sick."

"Then step outside, take a walk around the block." Tessa instructed her.

Sally stood up. "I should go with you."

"Do you mind if we take a break Tessa? Let us absorb everything." Annie asked.

"Sure. I'll clean up these dishes." Tessa stood up.

"That's a good idea, I'll help." Annie stood up with her.

"No, I've got it. You two relax." Tessa said carrying her dishes to the kitchen sink.

Annie got up and headed to the bathroom. David leaned back in his chair and watched Tessa as Lorna and Sally left through the kitchen door.

Tessa cleaned off all the dishes and loaded them into the dishwasher. She found her way to the second cabinet from the sink and opened it. She pulled out the plastic storage ware, filled them with leftovers, and placed them in the refrigerator. She soaked the remaining cooking pans with soapy water and proceeded to make a pot of coffee.

"You must have an incredible sense of direction and imagination." David offered.

Tessa brushed her hair back and wound her hair around a wrist tie as she sat back down. "I was sighted for 16 years. But yes, I do think I have an incredible imagination. Thank you for noticing."

"They can do eye transplants now, ever thought of it?"

"No. There are only so many eye transplants available in this world, and I don't need it like other people might. I couldn't live with myself if I took a pair of eyes, say, from a child. But speaking of imagination. You know, I've been doing this for about twenty years. I've done work for the intelligence agencies and several divisions of armed forces. All of that and not once did I ever have any security problems."

"Yeah, you were working *for* the security forces."

"My voice recognition software is used by corporations as well. I guess I just never imagined a problem. It's such a foolish move on Colby's part. I mean, I knew about the consortium so I may have just jumped to the conclusion it was Colby, or someone over at Sibley Systems. I beat him out of some pretty valuable contracts a couple of years back. I imagine this is payback. Why do you think it was Colby or do you? We never got around to talking about it."

"Yeah, same reasons. Who else would have any interest in what you're doing? I mean, I didn't mean it that way." David stumbled for an answer. "It just follows logic, Glen is ruthlessly trying to place Sibley at the top of the techno-security realm. Unfortunately, techno-security is a small universe. Even just the idea of something like this is in his reach and you can bet Glen Colby is going to want to get his hands on it. I think it was a crime of opportunity."

Tessa nodded. "Sounds more like a crime of passion, the way you describe Colby."

"Colby only has love for one. Himself."

Tessa smiled knowingly.

"Look, I want you to know I'm onboard with this, but I just," David feigned a shaky struggle in his voice, "I need to know if this goes south, you've got my best interest at heart just like you'd have for your sister."

Tessa could hear Annie's soft footsteps and raised her voice ever so slightly, hoping to ward off Annie. "David, in Watergate, the actual burglars got about a year in jail. Nixon had to resign and spent the rest of his life defending his shameful actions. I don't intend to spend a lifetime defending my actions and I don't intend on letting people who are acting for my benefit go to jail, ever. I would not send my sister or any of you into a trap. This is going to be easy, as long as you don't psych yourself out."

"I should have charged you a risk fee."

"I would have paid it, you'll have to assess that in the next audio interface I send you."

"It's a deal."

Annie walked in from the hallway. "Oh Tessa, you cleaned the whole kitchen!"

"And she did it blindfolded!" David offered.

Tessa laughed. Lorna and Sally popped back in through the kitchen door.

"See?" David reached over and touched Annie's neck. "Just another case for keeping women in the kitchen."

"What's so funny?" Sally asked, grabbing Lorna by the arm and jerking her back into the kitchen.

"David's on a roll." Annie grimaced.

Lorna searched Annie's face for a moment, she needed to get Annie away from him for a while. "Hey Annie, you think you might want to walk the dogs before we head out?"

"Yeah, I should. But let's go over this again. Make sure we're all on point and I'll do it when I go over to change clothes."

"What are you wearing?" Lorna asked.

"Her prom dress, come on *girls*, let's focus." David said.

Sally put her hand on Lorna's arm. "Honey, I'll get us some coffee, you have a seat."

Annie sat behind the wheel of her electric car scanning the roofs of the single story office park buildings. The question of which car to take was never even brought up, of course they'd take Annie's, this caper called for a very quiet car engine, not a high speed roadster. David and Lorna made last minute adjustments to their walkie-talkie earpieces and gear.

Annie lifted her walkie-talkie to her mouth. "Can you hear me?"

"OW!" David and Lorna popped out their earpieces.

"Annie, we're too close. Feedback, Dude." Lorna put her ear bud back in.

"Oh sorry."

Lorna held up a panty hose to the front seat for David. "Here."

"What is that?" David asked.

"A panty ho."

Annie giggled. "Just one."

"In case there are camera's." Lorna explained.

"I'm not wearing that." David said.

"Your choice. It's clean."

David put a ball cap on. "No thanks." And got out of the car.

Lorna pushed the passenger seat up and unfolded herself onto the street. She held out a pair of surgical gloves to David. "Fine, but if you don't put these on, then you're just looking to get caught."

David grabbed the gloves and stretched them onto his hands. Two street lamps down from them a lamp popped on, illuminating a large space in the parking lot.

"I'll be right here in twenty minutes." Annie said as Lorna quietly shut the car door.

Lorna looked through the double glass doors as they approached they approached the entrance. She could see a red and a green light shining from the alarm box on the inside wall.

David casually pulled a set of keys out of his pocket and held them up. He wore a Cheshire cat grin as he said, "Twenty dollars says my office building key will fit this one too."

Lorna felt the hair on the back of her neck prickle up. Keys or no keys, David was skipping their first step, which was to check the windows to make sure there was nobody inside. But she engaged with him anyway. "Twenty bucks says that door is already unlocked."

"You're on. These buildings are a crime against architecture." David continued his casual conversation.

"Hang on." David stopped short of the door. "Let's just go in, no one is going to be in there tonight and if someone shows up, I brought a friend."

Lorna, who was already peering in a small side window, swung around on him. David was holding a small revolver. The panty hose around her head and plastic gloves were making her feel claustrophobic and she began to sweat profusely. What if David tipped off Colby? Why didn't anyone think of this before? Her heart sank into her feet. She had to think of something to stall him, fast.

Tessa sat in the dark front room with Patience perched on her lap. Sally was in the kitchen, desperately trying to keep herself busy. She hated this waiting. This must be how defendants feel when the jury deliberates. The doorbell sounded its angelic cry shocking her to attention. She went out into the entryway and opened the front door. Two men in suits stood before her.

"Hello! I'm Glen Colby." The glossy one said.

From behind her Sally heard Tessa, "Glen! I'm so glad you could come by."

"David, wait. Something's wrong." Lorna moved further along the outer wall.

David held out the key for the door. "What?"

Lorna didn't answer but ran around the corner of the building.

Annie came over the earpiece. "Guys, the security truck is headed into the parking lot."

Lorna didn't respond, but she didn't see David either. She watched the truck lights do a circle around her and heard the truck drive off.

David appeared next to her. "Lucky maneuver, Kiddo. No thanks to Annie."

"That's your first mistake." Lorna followed him back around the front.

"What do you mean?"

"Do not underestimate Annie."

How did Tessa *not* think that David could be in cahoots with Colby? That's so very unlike Tessa. Her brain ricocheted with panic, was she walking into a trap? Why would he even think to bring a gun? "David, where's the master suite in these buildings?" Lorna knew the answer but stalled to think. Too many things were starting off wrong here. The green light shone on the alarm panel. Her mind scrambled back to what Sally had shown her when they went over how to hack into the panels. David suddenly had keys, a gun, and was skipping their first step. David was creating chaos.

"In the corners. They're corner offices but the way these buildings are laid out the corner offices are in the middle. We went over this." David acted exasperated.

"I need to go look in the windows then."

"Why?"

Lorna was already at a jog when she rounded the corner and began to look in the windows. David caught up with her. "Lorna stop. We don't have time for this."

"We'll make time." She said and kept moving from one dark window to the next. Lorna wedged herself behind the hedgerow to get closer to the darkened building windows.

"Fine. I'll go around the other side and meet you back at the door." David said.

Lorna moved along the building and hit her shin on something metal and sharp sticking out from the building. She gasped and stifled a cry. Pulling out her flashlight, she looking down. The tall windowpane had a bottom panel that opened out into the hedgerow. She pushed down on the window and it opened another inch further. She didn't even look around or take a moment to think if she could make it through the opening. She took her jacket, walkie-talkie and headset off and slid in feet first.

Once she was inside, she immediately put her gear back on and closed the window. The metallic canned air in the room was thick with stale carpet smell. She scanned the office as her eyes adjusted to the dark. How can she warn Annie away? She opened the office door and stepped out into the sea of low-sided cubicles in front of her.

She pushed the talk button on her walkie-talkie. "Guys, I'm in. There's someone here. David, fall back."

David's voice popped on in her ear. "What? How'd you get in?"

"A window." She said, but kept moving rapidly around looking at the door nameplates for Colby's office.

"Then get out, Lorna!" Annie cried.

"No, he's wearing earphones, he can't hear me." She stopped in front of Colby's office, the door was locked, but there was nothing like a high-tech encrypto thingy. It was just a locked door. She needed a paperclip or a thick piece of plastic.

"Which window?" David asked.

She looked at the desk directly in front of Colby's office. Wait a minute. Don't these rooms have movable walls? She looked up and went over into the next office. She looked at the name on the door. Paul Owens. Lorna's mind raced back to the story Annie had told about David's friend, Paul. "Son, ofabitch." Lorna muttered and pulled off her panty hose.

"Lorna?" David said again.

"Hang on. Look, at some point he's going to have to use the bathroom. I'll let you in when he does."

"I'm coming around to your side."

A paralyzing thought blindsided her. What if this Paul Owens is in here somewhere? She immediately rejected the thought. No, but David must be in on this. I don't know how but he's been in on this from the beginning. "Keep moving forward." She muttered. She pushed the talk button again. "Okay, good, I'll let you in when the coast is clear." Lorna put her hand over the lens of the flashlight, only letting a few rays shine through her fingers.

Lorna looked around. If it was me, she thought, and I wanted to steal this thing I would hide it in Colby's office, just in case, that way it will look like Colby stole it.

Lorna left Paul's office door and went over to the desk in front of Colby's office and opened the top drawer. She lifted up a pencil tray and pulled out the key. She turned around and unlocked Colby's door. The smell of men's aftershave accosted her and she chocked back a cough. Using her flashlight she looked around frantically. Desk, chair, credenza, guest chairs, he doesn't even have a computer. Lorna rolled her eyes. She went over to the credenza and got down on her knees to open it. It was locked. Lorna's head dropped to the side in frustration, "I've got no—". A dangling piece of tape was caught in her flashlight beam. She looked up at the underside of the desk drawer. Something was taped to it. It's about the right size, she thought. She reached up and pulled it off the drawer bottom. She put her flashlight on the floor next to it. Opening the case, she looked down at the contents, it was exactly as Tessa described.

A distant squeak scratched through the heavy air. She stopped moving. Lorna shoved the plastic box in her underwear, just in case.

"Lorna," David whispered over the headset. "I'm coming in."

"Good timing, hurry and I'll meet you there." She said scrambling up.

She grabbed the key from the cabinet and locked the door back. She tossed the key back into the opposite desk's top drawer.

Lorna took long strides down the aisle to the door where she first came in. She met David at the door. "Come on, hurry. Three offices down on the right."

David hustled straight to the desk in front of Colby's office and threw open the top drawer. He didn't even hesitate as he lifted the key out. Lorna pretended to be looking over at the other cubicles around the room.

When he opened the door she offered, "I'll stand watch, you look around."

David went directly behind the desk to the credenza, but he bent down and she couldn't tell if he was looking under the desk or not.

"Come on David," she whispered urgently.

"I'm looking. I need a paperclip or something. Wait, I've got one." David slid open the credenza.

Lorna listened to the noises he was making but kept her gaze over the mass of cubicles on the other side. She suppressed the urge to run out of the office building. "He's leaving." She said softly.

"Good." David whispered.

"Annie?" Lorna said into the walkie-talkie. "I need you to make another trip around the block and then meet us back here. Okay?"

"Got it." Annie responded.

"I don't see anything." David continued looking around.

Lorna looked back at him. David's movements had become and frantic and jerky. He knocked a pile of papers off the desk.

Lorna interceded. "David, stop. You're getting careless." She came over and lifted the papers off the floor and neatened them as best she could back on the desk.

"Look, if it's not here, it's not here. We did the best we could."

"Oh you're not going to give up that easy, Darlin'." David sneered.

"Yes, I am. Sally said 'first and foremost don't get caught'. If that guy is leaving now then he's going to be setting the alarm as he goes. We have to get out of here. We can come back tomorrow night too or go to the boat."

Lorna opened the office door but David was still standing behind the desk looking around. "Hey, if you get caught now, it's your business." She said before turning to leave.

But David fell in step with her at the third office down. "Yeah, Tessa was *so* sure it was here, wasn't she? Colby's not stupid, he's probably got it on that boat he stay's on."

Lorna pushed her talk button. "Annie, you out there?"

"Almost."

David pushed open the window. "Ladies first."

They rode back to Saint Charles Place under a dark cloud. David didn't stop talking the whole way. 'This was stupid, of course he wouldn't leave it in his office. How could she send in her own sister? Now, what is she going to do.' And on and on. Annie kept an eye on Lorna in the rearview mirror, expecting her fuse to blow any second. But Lorna seemed to be ignoring him, lost in her own thoughts, as she watched out the window.

Annie turned her car into the driveway but Lorna couldn't keep her eyes off her own house across the street.

"Don't get out yet." She said, peering through the car's back window.

"Why?" David wanted to know.

"Because, Sally never leaves every light in the house blazing like that and Tessa doesn't need them. Someone is in there."

"What do we do?" Annie asked.

"We should go see." David said getting out of the car.

Annie and Lorna followed. The front door to their house swung open. Lorna dove behind the car leaving Annie and David standing there like a couple of deer in the headlights. A couple of men came out to the front porch followed by Sally.

"Shit, it's Colby." David said under his breath and turned away from the street. He stood in front of Annie. "Kiss me."

"No." Annie said.

"Just kiss me, so they'll think we're kissing."

"I don't want to kiss you."

"Kiss him Annie!" Lorna hissed from behind the car.

Annie begrudgingly wrapped her arms around David's neck. "No tongue."

David leaned into the kiss, as the men climbed into a car parked not twenty feet away and drove off. Once they turned onto the main road David pulled back and Lorna stood up. "That wasn't so bad." He said softly to Annie.

"It was for me." Lorna said walking by. "I had to witness it."

Annie said nothing, but turned to walk across the street with Lorna.

Sally was turning out the front room lights as Lorna, Annie, and David walked in. Sally met them at the door. "Where's Tessa?" Lorna asked.

"Kitchen." Sally was able say as Lorna marched past her. "How'd it go?" Sally stood in front of David.

"Not good I'm afraid." He said as they made their way to the kitchen behind Lorna.

Tessa was holding Lorna's hand between her own when they walked in. Tessa released her hand and Lorna sat down. "I know, I was afraid of that." She was saying.

"Why was Colby here?" David demanded.

"Gloating, I suppose." Tessa shrugged. "Apparently, he heard I had arrived early to the island and wanted to meet me."

"What the hell?" David sat down lost in thought. "Who was with him?"

Tessa smiled. "His attorney. Thank you guys. Thank you for trying so hard."

"That's so brazen!" Annie exclaimed.

"Well, people don't get to where Colby is by not being *so brazen*." Tessa nodded.

Annie was shocked. This is not the woman she had come to know. She looked to Lorna and Sally for a sign, but they were straight faced showing no emotion. Sally's somber attention was on Tessa and Lorna stared at the table.

"I'm just so glad you got out okay. No troubles?"

"No." Lorna spoke up. "We were in and out."

"Tessa, I'm so sorry." Annie said.

"Thank you. But you win some, you lose some."

"What are you going to tell your client?" Annie asked.

"Well, David, do you feel like making another audio interface?"

David, who had been lost in his thoughts, snapped to attention. "You're going to make *another* one?"

"Of course. I have to meet the clients needs."

David shook his head. "I don't know. Let me think about it?"

"Sure." Tessa smiled.

Lorna wanted him out before his mistake dawned on him and said. "Annie, you look tired. I'm kaput."

Sally took the cue and stood up. "Right, why don't we rehash this in the morning."

David took the signal willingly. "I hope you don't mind if I bow out."

Tessa stood up. "I completely understand David."

"Annie, I'll see you again I hope?" David said as he made his way out of the room.

"Of course." She said as Sally showed David to the door.

Annie started to leave but Lorna reached over and grabbed her arm and stopped her. Lorna put her finger to her own lips to hush Annie. Annie nodded and heard the door shut.

Lorna sat back down and turned to Tessa. "I want a drink."

Tessa stood up. "Point me in the right direction."

"Bottom cabinet, sink side, first on the left."

Tessa went over to it and fumbled her way around. She held a bottle up. "What is it?" She said as Sally came back in to the room.

"Bourbon." they said in unison.

Sally grabbed some glasses, put them on the table. Then reached over and grabbed Tessa's remote control key fob from the counter and flicked on the frequency jammer.

Annie watched as Lorna pulled the kitchen curtains closed. Sally walked out of the kitchen door, looked around outside and come back in, shutting the door behind her.

Tessa splashed bourbon into the glasses and held up a glass. "To you beautiful, wonderful women."

Annie held up her glass in confusion. "I don't understand."

Lorna laughed and let out a long vocal sigh. "Aaaaah, yeah, neither do I." She took a long swig of her bourbon. "But." Lorna reached into her pants and yanked something. She grunted loudly, "Ahhh!" And screwed her face up as she pulled out a small box. "I have this!" She put the box, with the tape, and now some short-curlies still attached, on the table and pointed to it. "You may want to wash that first."

"Ew. Lorna!" Sally said.

Annie stood up. She was at once, confused, enthralled and terrified. "I would like to know what is going on!" She sat back down.

"Where was it?" Tessa demanded, her hands stretching out for the box on the table.

Sally grabbed the box first. "In her pants! Here, let me get it out for you." Sally carefully pulled out the device and set it in front of Tessa.

"No where was it before?" Tessa clarified.

"Taped under Colby's desk. But David made the mistake of knowing where the key to his desk was hidden."

Tessa patted the table with finality. "David tried to steal it. It was David. When I jumped to the conclusion Colby had stolen it, it was a viable idea, and it was perfect for him. Colby does have a 'by hook or by crook' reputation, and given the right circumstances my accusation could very well have been true, but it wasn't. One reason I chose David for the audio interface was his close proximity to the island. He lives *and* works here. What I learned tonight and what David doesn't know yet, is that Landsea and Glen's company, Sibley, are merging. That's what all those emails were referring to, Annie. There's no reason for Colby to steal this. When I kept pursuing my plans though, I imagine David felt threatened. So instead of getting caught out right he took a chance and tried to frame his friend's boss. But I had no way of proving that, it was just a theory. When did you figure it out Lorna?"

"I didn't. Thank you so very much. Something didn't feel right when we were walking to the door," Lorna began and went through everything that had happened at the office building. "Why didn't you just tell me?" She finally asked Tessa.

Tessa scoffed. "Because I'd rather bail you out of jail for a botched robbery than attempted murder. I knew if you got too close, he'd give himself away and you'd put it together. No one has instincts as good as yours."

Annie looked at Sally. "Did you know?"

"No." Sally looked wide-eyed. "I almost crapped when the doorbell rang and that guy introduced himself as Glenn Colby."

"Now that," Tessa nodded, "was underhanded of me. I invited Colby over, under the pretense of having a drink together now that I'm in town for a couple of days. I figured if he was here, he certainly wouldn't be at his office or his yacht. It was the only thing I could think of to protect you in case I was wrong about David. It could have gone either way."

Annie put her bourbon down. "Tessa, y' know, I just want to go down on record as saying I think that was wrong of you to withhold information from us. Especially Lorna. You could have put her in a very dangerous situation. And I had to *kiss* him."

Lorna couldn't help but change the subject. "What do you bet that he's on the phone right now with his buddy Paul, accusing him of double crossing him."

Annie turned to Sally. "Am I wrong Sally?"

"No, you're not. Tessa, it was careless. You suspected David and didn't say a word about it. It simply stupid luck that Lorna found this. You didn't even know David had hidden it in Colby's office. But you went on and sent Lorna and Annie into that situation."

Tessa carefully placed her hands around the device. "There are only two people at Landsea that knew what I was putting together. The CEO and the CFO. The CEO is friends with Quill, so I know for a fact neither one of them had said a word about it. So, yes, I was taking a chance. But it was a calculated one. There is no way David even knew what he was stealing. Not until I told him." Tessa took a sip of her Bourbon. "But you're right. I should have found a moment to fill you in. I'm sorry. I acted like a puppet master. Anything could have happened and I should have given you at least the courtesy of knowing the ideas I was working from."

They sat for a moment in silence. Finally Lorna spoke up. "This is crap. Whatever the hell happened, it worked out. We got it back. Done. And I'd like to feel happy about that." Lorna lifted her glass. "To me!"

Annie was not at all amused and she stood up. "Is this nut bag going to come after us now?"

"No." Sally spoke with assurance. "David had his chance tonight. Which is scary enough to think about. But, what I've learned with criminals like David, is he's an opportunist. I understand what Tessa is saying now. He had an opportunity to take something, but when the heat got too much he saw a way out of it. Self-preservation. He probably didn't even know he was giving it back, he was unconsciously protecting himself."

"That's very true, I think. When you and Lorna went for that walk earlier David said something about Colby just committing a crime of opportunity. Someone like Glen Colby does not commit crimes of opportunity like this. David was talking about himself. David *knew* I was flying in early. And, I'm guessing here but, I think he must have rode by the house, saw the package, and took it. Then when he found out what was inside, I'll bet he panicked. It may have been subconscious but I think he was looking for a way to give it back."

"You mean like a survival instinct?" Annie asked.

"Maybe." Tessa said.

Lorna wanted to change the subject off David. She would broach the subject of David's gun and Tessa's carelessness in this whole affair privately. In a small and slurred voice she squeeked, "Paris."

"Oh Lorna, you think so small sometimes." Tessa admonished her. "I'm talking big, life altering, fresh start kind of appreciation for Annie."

"What do you mean?" Annie asked.

Tessa put a hand across the table to Annie. "You're going through such a big change and I want to help. Just think about what you'd like to be doing in a few years. Perhaps you'd like to make some new goals for yourself. I know Lorna could really use some help marketing that book of hers." Tessa shrugged. "It's a standing offer."

"Think about it in Paris." Lorna pushed.

"Fine!" Tessa leaned her head up toward the ceiling. "She can think about it in Paris. I'll call my travel agent tomorrow."

CHAPTER 8

Parent sTrap

Sunday morning came and went with Sally reading through Annie's 'internet divorce' papers, Tessa working on her presentation, and Lorna sleeping it off. After Lorna got up she read the morning paper and ate breakfast with the usual languidness befitting a Sunday morning, except it was now early afternoon. Sally watched as Lorna got up from the kitchen table and walked back to her office, where Tessa was working, and heard her quietly shut the door.

"Good morning, sleepy head." Tessa said from the desk.

Lorna sunk into her reading chair.

"Every morning I awake is a good morning." Lorna said cheerlessly.

"Uh oh."

"I didn't say anything before in front or everyone but David brought a gun to our little dalliance last night."

"Oh my God."

"Yeah. And here's the thing, I know you have an image to uphold. I get that. I don't exactly know what information you withheld - some kind of something, I don't know. But there is no way you could have guessed that David took your package from the front porch. And there is no *way* you could have known that he put it back into Colby's office. But whatever, it all worked out so I don't care. I do care that you put *me* in danger. Your own sister."

"I had no idea he would—"

"I don't care what you have as an explanation now, it's after the fact. You've been acting like a real shit-head for a while now. You got Dad to put in a frequency jammer and God knows what else in *my* home and now this thing. So I don't know what you are really getting up to in your business lately but you are going to keep Sally and me out of it from now on. All these little secrets and lies you're playing around with are going to get someone hurt. Sally and Annie think the world of you and that's great. I'm glad we can all be friends but this shit you're doing now, all these secrets are corrosive and destructive so no more. It's one thing for you to manipulate me but you need to keep the rest of the family out of it."

"I'm sorry."

"Is there anything else I need to know? About my home or anything else about David? Is this now going to be a *thing* I need to worry about?"

"No. I assure you it won't be."

"Uh huh." Lorna got up and quietly let herself back out of the room.

Annie had dinner with them that evening. Then she and Sally went over the divorce papers making additions and taking out lines Sally felt were either too general or could be too easily appealed. Somewhere along the way

Lorna agreed to help Annie start packing up Tim's things from the house, since he hadn't bothered to show up and do it himself. Which is why, the next day, for the second time in as many weeks she found herself doing Annie's housework.

Lorna stood back from the now empty bedroom closet and looked over at the three medium size boxes and one hanging clothes box, and sighed. She considered the nightstand on Tim's side of the bed. No, she reconsidered; Annie had only asked that she cleared out Tim's side of the closet. Lorna grabbed the hanging clothes box, carried it downstairs into the dining room, and placed it down next to the only box Annie had packed from the office in the last three hours. At the rate Annie is packing, she thought to herself, this is never going to happen.

Lorna found Annie back in her office. "Hey."

Annie looked up from her computer. "Hey, I'm sorry, I've just gotten so behind with work. I don't see how I can complete these – I just don't know, you'd think someone would see how much I *wasn't* doing and step in!"

"Annie. I've got this, it's okay, and you just keep working. I'm going to forage for some lunch. How about a peanut butter and jelly?"

"That's great." Annie smiled in relief.

"Do you want me to keep going and like, empty out Tim's night stand? I don't want to step on any boundaries or anything. But he still has his toiletries and stuff"

"No. That's fine. I don't care, that's his problem." Annie cut her off.

Lorna backed away nodding and made her way back to the kitchen. Annie had gone from desperate to joyful, at the peanut butter and jelly sandwich, to passive aggressive in less than a minute. That's all she needed to know about Annie's state of mind. Had she done the right thing by pushing Annie through this? But then again, she did find

Annie in an emotional cesspool four days ago. Maybe it was a mistake to include her in on this past weekend's activities. But how did anyone, except maybe Tessa, know it was going to turn out like that? Annie needed time to process everything that was happening that, Lorna thought. Annie needed to feel some modicum of control in her life. Since she can't control this divorce thing, then maybe she'll feel some control in her work life. Lorna looked over at the shelves in the living room filled with c.d.'s and movies and thought, *now that*, Annie will have to go through by herself.

As Lorna put together the sandwiches, she pulled her cell phone from her pocket and speed dialed Sally at work.

"Hey."

"Hi, Honey." Sally sounded busy.

"I just wanted you to know, it looks like I'm going to be spending my day here with Annie."

"Okay." Sally said absent-mindedly.

"I'm going to call you again at 3:00."

"Sounds good." Sally varied her response.

"Have you heard from Tessa?"

"No."

"And do you want a knuckle sandwich for dinner?"

"Mmm, that sounds good can I have slap-slaw with it?"

Lorna giggled. "Talk later."

They hung up and Lorna finished the sandwiches. She was also worried about Tessa and her meeting in San Francisco. Something didn't feel right with Tessa during this whole visit. The fact that Silicon Valley and San Francisco are probably the safest places in the world for Tessa Tollison of TollComm, didn't make her worry any less for her sister. If Tessa was using bad judgment, reckless even, with her own sister than what kind of judgment is she using with her business?

Lorna walked into the office where Annie continued typing at a ferocious rate. "Lunch."

"Thank you, Lorna." Annie called out to her as she continued typing.

"You're welcome." Called back as she made her way back to the dining room for another box to take upstairs. It's one o'clock now, she thought, if she spends another hour finishing the upstairs and two hours taking care of his personal effects downstairs, it should put a huge dent in the actual physical work Annie will have to handle. And if he ever does show up again, then maybe doing all this will curtail any superfluous arguments they might get into.

She grabbed the daily newspaper off the coffee table and took it with her to wrap up any breakables she would have to pack. She had thought that by going through his things like this that maybe she'd glean a reason why Tim would suddenly want a divorce from Annie. Maybe a stray bottle of aftershave would indicate a torrid romance. A large secret stash of pornographic magazines, cash, or even lingerie receipts but so far nothing to changed her mind about Tim. He's really is just the boy next door.

She sat on the edge of the bed and opened the nightstand drawer. She lifted up a sheet of the newspaper to wrap up Tim's alarm clock and looked at the newspaper headline: Silicon Suicide. She read on. A Silicon Valley entrepreneur, Brian Hodge, who had relocated his company, The Hayward, to Hayward, California was found dead in his offices on Sunday. The police are ruling it a suicide. Hodge's company produced mapping software and had recently been bought by Spectorgies for ten million dollars. But he had planned to stay on at the helm of the company. "What is wrong with these people?" Lorna said aloud. A spokesperson for Spectorgies expressed their surprise and condolences to Hodges' family. She shook her head disapprovingly. Perhaps Annie was right and this whole thing could be blamed on his job with Spectorgies.

Lorna thought about the Borg from the *Star Trek* television series that abducted and assimilated people into 'the collective'. Maybe it makes good business sense but for Lorna Spectorgies is like the Borg now, instead of having competition or just licensing software, they just buy the source. Lorna wrapped the alarm clock in the paper. Ten million dollars for mapping software, what is the mapping software for? Middle Earth?

What Sally didn't know about the historic Fairmont Hotel that perches atop of the Nob Hill district in San Francisco was it was the brainchild of sisters, Tessie and Virginia Fair. She knew it had survived the 1906 earthquake and was where they drafted the 1945 United Nations Charter. But when she looked up the address in the computer she also found out about the Fair sisters and after the earthquake it was refinished and structurally reinforced by a female architect and engineer, Julia Morgan. Morgan had been the first woman to graduate with a degree in architecture from the Ecole des Beaux Arts in Paris. The story made her smile. Yet she was even more impressed when she saw the hotel.

Sally pulled the car over to the loading zone where she could see Tessa's orange mop of hair flapping in unison with the flags that lined the building. The handsome, physically fit older man that was standing next to her was dressed formally in a double-breasted suit, unusual for a Silicon Valley type. Sally waved at the man indicating she was Tessa's ride. The man held the door out for Tessa and they said their goodbyes.

"So?" Sally wanted to know as she pulled the car back out in traffic and onto Mason Street.

"Not a single hitch. Everything went as planned and we are in good stead."

"Good."

"I can't wait to get home."

"Me too…I mean me. *I* can't wait to get home."

"Wasn't exactly a restful weekend was it?" Tessa acknowledged.

"No."

"Yeah, sorry about that. Lorna's very mad at me about it."

"She is?" Sally was genuinely surprised.

"I've been a shit. According to my sister. But I don't think she's wrong. I was manipulative and didn't need to be. I hope I didn't cause irreparable damage, I hope you can still trust me."

"You mean about my past with the CIA?"

"With anything."

"Sure." Sally replied casually. Had she given Tessa too much credit in the deception department? She just didn't trust Tessa's humbled veneer.

"I'm glad. I guess I'm still new to working with these high profile gadgets, well, not the gadgets but the people who want them. I really made some mistakes and over shot my goal. Did Lorna tell you David had brought a gun to the, uh, proceedings?"

Sally shook her head no. "No, but it was smart not to tell me. Don't you think?" Sally sidestepped Tessa's bait. Why is Tessa so bound and determined to drive a wedge between Lorna and me?

"There's one more thing I wanted to talk with you about though, this divorce between Annie and Tim."

"What about it?"

"Do you remember when Lorna told me about Tim's company being bought out by Spectorgies?"

"Not really, but go ahead."

"Well, anyway. There are two things. One, Spectorgies holds a lot of defense contracts with the government, namely with the NSA. And two, my friend –

the one I contacted about seeing if he had any pull with Spectorgies? He works for the NSA. Which is why I'm worried."

"I don't get it, I don't see how one has to do with the other."

"Last I heard, it was Tim's IT human resources team, the Geek Squad he called them, that were the only ones left after Spectorgies basically gutted the human resource personnel and put in their own people. Which could mean the NSA pressured Spectorgies to keep them all on so they'd have their little informants in place."

"So you think Tim started working for the NSA as an informant while working for Spectorgies?"

"I'm starting to. As you know, doing that sort of thing changes people – being deceptive like that. And as a human resource analyst he's in the perfect position to see the coming and goings of Silicon Valley's brain trust of engineers, technicians, and scientists. He'd know about who is being brought in for projects, what specialists were needed where, and what all that means. It would be a good fit in the intelligence gathering for the NSA."

"But, if the NSA is basically the customer for Spectorgies, shouldn't Spectorgies kiss their ass?"

"You'd think, but no. There are a lot more customers they could cater to, weapons traffickers, other countries, and rebel forces in where-the-hell-ever. I'm telling you intelligence and gathering is the new 'it' product out there. And I think I may have put Tim in the middle of the soup. Which would explain his bizarre behavior and maybe this divorce."

Sally took a deep breath and thought about this. It is not like Tessa to take to hyperbole. "Can't you just check with your friend?"

"No, that NSA is just a one way communication hole. Even between friends."

"Well, do you want to talk with Tim?"

"I don't know.   One reason why he'd push his wife away like he has is if he'd gotten in over his head. Ya' know, he'd push her away in the name of protecting her."

"But that is *so* not the Tim I knew."

"I don't think that either. But if you say 'it's not the Time you know' then you'd have to ask who is the Tim you do know. Why did you hide your CIA background from Lorna?"

"Because I was ashamed."

"Well, there you have it. Self-preservation again. Like David."

Sally thought about this for a moment. Tessa did have a point. "I hate to say this aloud, but I don't really want to get involved with this."

"A little too close to home?"

"Yes. I'm just getting used to the idea of trusting *you*."

"Be that as it may, I feel a little responsible. Any chance of you maybe having a conversation with him?"

"No, I'm sorry."

"Wait, I don't mean you exposing yourself, I mean could you get a message to him to contact me?"

"Oh sure, I could do that."

"Just keep it on the down low, Lorna and Annie don't need to know I'm in contact with him. It'll look like I'm playing both sides."

Sally laughed. "And you're not?"

"Of course I am, but they don't need to know that."

Lorna brought the last box down from the upstairs and placed it in the dining room with the others when Annie walked in.

"How's it going?" Lorna asked.

"That's a lot of shit." Annie said looking at the stacks of boxes.

"I didn't realize he had so many shoes." Lorna said patting a box. "An entire box of shoes, I don't even have that many shoes."

"We're going to need more boxes." Annie nodded.

"Are you taking a break?" Lorna asked hopefully.

"No, well yes. I need the newspaper."

"Oh. I'm sorry. I wrapped the stuff from his nightstand in it. You can use mine, it's at my house."

"Don't worry about it. Do you need it back?" Annie moved toward the front door.

"No. My keys are on your coffee table."

"Okay, I'll be right back." She shut the door behind her.

Lorna mumbled, "Don't worry, I'll put your dogs outside," and assembled another box.

As Annie walked across the street, she wondered why the owners of the Auld Alliance Café were sitting on Lorna and Sally's front steps. They returned her little wave and smiled broadly as she approached them.

"Hi." Annie said noncommittally.

The elderly lady sprung up from the stairs. "Hello, again. I remember you from the café, you're Lorna's friend."

Annie knitted her eyebrows together. "Yes."

The lady tapped her chest excitedly. "Do you know when they get home?"

"No. Um, probably not until after five o'clock." Annie lied. She was stunned but couldn't figure out what they wanted. The old man just sat there, sprawled across the stairs, enjoying the sun on his face and looking over at Annie's house. She wanted to go inside and get that newspaper so she could finish her market research presentation but these two were acting weird, like they had some dominion over Lorna and Sally's front steps.

Annie carefully walked up the stairs past them and the lady followed her. "We're the Baumgarten's. I'm Eunice and this is Wallace."

Annie stopped at the front door. "I just need to pick up the newspaper." Annie felt frustrated by the irrational need to explain herself. She wasn't staying, she couldn't exactly invite them in, and they weren't explaining themselves to her.

Eunice moved in on Annie's personal space and touched her elbow. "We're Sally's parents."

Annie's mouth opened to speak. "But." She took a step back from Eunice. "But." Five thoughts hit her at once. She struggled to make one of those thoughts into a question. Sally's parents are dead. Who are these people? Why would the café owners be Sally's parents? Is Sally a run away? She finally asked, "Does Sally know?"

"Well yes, I suppose she would." Eunice answered.

"Why didn't you just call Sally?" Annie asked.

"It's complicated. Can we come in?" Eunice asked, holding open the screen door.

"No. I mean. Yes, but could you hang on a minute?" Annie made her way down the steps. "I'll be right back."

Annie ran across the street and flung open her own front door. Lorna was standing in the front room staring at the shelves. "You need to go home right now." Annie blurted out.

"What?" Lorna scowled. "Is it the cops?" Or had Annie finally gone off the deep end.

"You need to go home. Now."

"What the fuck?" Lorna wanted to know.

"I can't. Don't ask questions, come on."

"Are you coming with me?"

Annie's eyebrows rose to great heights. "Oh yeah."

As they crossed the street Lorna looked over at Annie and spoke out of the side of her mouth. "Are those the café owners?"

"Yup." Annie said then pursed her lips together.

"Hi," Lorna started.

Annie interrupted. "We should go inside." She pulled the front door keys from her pocket and let them all inside.

Lorna moved into the doorway and stopped, crossing her arms in front of her and planting her feet down. "What's going on?" She demanded.

"Lorna, meet Eunice and Wallace Baumgarten," Annie voice came out in a singsong fashion, "*Sally's parents*."

Lorna's eyebrows raised up and she automatically stuck her hand out. "Nice to meet you."

"Hello!" Wallace barked out.

"Wallace!" Eunice yelled and tapped at her ears before turning back to Lorna. "It's so nice to finally meet you."

Wallace reached his hands up to his ears and clicked on his hearing aids.

Annie took charge because Lorna looked like she could have been knocked over by a feather. "Won't you come in and have a seat?"

They moved to the living room and sat down. "I thought you were dead." Lorna said.

"Only on paper." Eunice explained.

Lorna looked at both of them. "This is crazy. Why would you claim to be Sally's parents and not contact her? I mean, I don't understand."

"We have a lot of making up to do to our poor Sally." Eunice frowned.

"My mother raised her." Wallace added loudly.

Eunice jumped back in. "You see we worked abroad a good deal and it was just easier, but we're retired now and ready to settle down. So we opened the café."

Annie asked, "You retired to open a business?"

"Well sure." Wallace barked. "What are we suppose to do sit around and rot?"

"The rotting is preventable. Most people knit or play golf." Annie countered.

"Annie." Lorna stopped the banter. "Why would you say you were dead, on paper?"

Eunice and Wallace had no idea how much Lorna actually knew about them so Eunice fielded the question. "We got involved with some security matter's overseas and it was simply easier to be dead. Oh, but we've been in New Zealand for the past five or six years, until the heat was off."

Annie giggled to herself. Lorna scowled at Annie. "Didn't you come for a newspaper?"

"It can wait." Annie said nodding assuredly.

Lorna could not think of a reason why anyone would claim to be Sally's parents. It was just so random. "What about your mother?" Lorna asked Wallace.

"She's doing great. Sally did a fantastic job getting her settled in." Wallace smiled.

"We've had that place picked out for quite a while now. They have a wonderful reputation." Eunice agreed.

Lorna put her head down in her hand. "I'm sorry. This is a lot to process."

Annie asked the obvious question. "Why would Sally lie about this?"

"She didn't lie." Eunice drew out.

"She did." Wallace said. "But she had to. She even changed her last name, the little whippersnapper."

"Well, I mean, do you think she's going to be *happy* to see you now?"

Eunice exchanged a knowing glance with Wallace and said, "I can't imagine why not?"

Something was wrong here. Lorna could feel it in her bones. They aren't telling her the truth. "Why did it take you so long to contact her? Why not do it in Phoenix, at Grandma Souchek's?" Then it dawned on Lorna as the name Souchek left her lips. Maybe because Grandma wouldn't recognize them, or because they weren't wanted there. The only thing Lorna knew for sure right now was that these people were lying.

"We were busy with the café." Eunice's answer was pat.

Lorna took a beat looking into Eunice and Wallace's smiling faces, then over to Annie's eager grin and changed tactics. She stood up. "Can I get anyone anything to drink?"

"Just some water would be fine." Wallace said leaning back in his seat.

Annie got up from the couch. "Lorna, I should go. Let me get that newspaper, the kitchen probably…" Annie's voice trailed off as she left following Lorna into the kitchen.

Once they scrambled into the kitchen together Annie asked, "Do you want me to stay?"

Lorna pulled a couple of glasses down from the cabinet. "No, I'll handle them."

"Okay." Annie grabbed the newspaper up from the table.

"But come back later, okay?"

"Of course." Annie said leaving.

Lorna went back in to the living room with the water's and set the glasses down on the coffee table in front of Eunice and Wallace. Wallace craned his neck around as he watched Annie make her way back across the street.

Lorna shook her head at them. "I think this is awful, it's like you're sandbagging Sally. Why don't you go back to the café or where ever you live and I'll let Sally know you're in town?"

"We can't."

Lorna's heart sank. Are they homeless? "Why?"

"Well, Sally's in danger and we're here to protect her." The elderly woman explained.

"Start from the beginning Margaret!" Wallace yelled.

Who's Margaret? Lorna thought.

"We retired from the CIA. That's why—" Eunice began.

Wallace interrupted again. "Look, your friends over there from across the street are dragging Sally back into something she doesn't want to be involved in. They've hired a mercenary!"

Lorna's mouth fell open. "What? Annie and Tim?"

"My mother thought it would be a good idea to get Sally to do some aid work in Bosnia before she went to law school. Turns out it was a CIA recruitment camp and our Sally must have drawn a short straw because she ends up shooting a traitor. That's why she hates us. But we're still her parents, we still have to protect her."

Lorna looked around for something to hang on to, even though she was sitting on the couch. She said slowly, "Sally's – a - spy."

"No. Who said anything about a spy?" Eunice wanted to know.

"Okay." Lorna put her hand up and tried again, "Sally's a fugitive?"

"From what?" Wallace asked.

"You said she shot a man. Was she convicted?"

"No! It was in Bosnia. Self-defense. There were witnesses and everything. It was a clear-cut case."

"So, forgive me, but why are you here?"

"Pickles." Eunice said.

"Pickles had always kept us filled in on our little girl, but things were heating up around here and so Pickles called us in." Wallace finished what Eunice began.

Lorna looked over at Eunice for clarification.

"He was a good friend of ours and now he's dead." Eunice explained.

"Pickles?"

"Yes."

"So Pickles called you back from New Zealand and said, 'It's getting hot on Ohlone Island where your daughter, who killed a man, lives and you should go there.'"

"Yes. But then he died." Eunice nodded.

"And Sally doesn't know anything about this?"

"We don't know. That's why we're here now."

"Okay," Lorna struggled to organize her thoughts. "Can we get back to this mercenary thing?"

"Of course, Dear." Eunice smiled enigmatically.

CHAPTER 9

HE WHO TRAVELS

"He travels the fastest who travels alone!"
Kipling

What in the world is happening? Annie sat back down in her office chair and stared at her computer, lost in her thoughts, for another minute. She dialed Sally's cell phone again. And again it went straight to Sally's voice mail. "Sally. It's Annie. Please call me when you get this. When you get home, can you come over to my house first? Just call me when you get this." Annie ended the phone call and put her phone back down. What in the world is going on around here? It's like Saturn is in retrograde or something. She picked up the phone again to call Tim, but inhaled sharply and set the phone back down. He doesn't want to talk to me, she thought. Sadness consumed her momentarily before she stopped it abruptly. First Tim and now Sally.

"No. What do I *need*?" She asked herself aloud. "I *need* to finish my work so I don't get fired." She answered rightly. Lorna is going to need her help later so she better get all of her work done first, she thought, and turned back to her computer.

Roberta just could not leave this alone. The same innate forces that made Roberta a detective were drawing her to the Lemon Sud. She knew she could not influence what the FBI or Tim would do here, but what she'd really like is for them to do it somewhere else. She parked her cruiser on the other side of the block and got out to walk the rest of the way to the safe house. She hated the fact that she even knew the FBI kept a safe house on the island because it's like a mosquito bite you can't leave alone.

The smell of rotting wood and stale beer was daunting. Roberta was wearing one of her new suits and frankly she didn't want to deal with a dry cleaning bill on her first day. She climbed the rickety stairs carefully to the floor above the Lemon Sud carrying a small bag of groceries. Michael opened the door for her.

"Thanks." Michael tried to take the bag from her but she pulled it back.

"This isn't for *you*. I got three kids to feed at home. Get your own food." She looked around the apartment. "Where's Tim?"

"He took off. While I was sleeping this afternoon."

Roberta recognized the desperation in his eyes from when Keeling pulled him out of the estuary after the boat bomb.

Michael added, "He saw the newspaper. And he's got a gun."

"What kind of gun?"

"His Dad's old service revolver.'"

"He's that scared?"

"Brian Hodge was murdered."

"Who's that?"

"Hodges, from The Hayward. Where Tim got the Aurora?"

"Oh." Roberta searched her memory. "That was ruled a suicide."

"Come on." Michael implored. "I have looked everywhere for him, our old meet ups, places I'd heard him talk about, those empty boats along the estuary, our surveillance van."

"You two have a surveillance van?"

"Of course. Do you have any idea how many places there are to hide on this island?"

"Did you check his house?"

Michael shook his head no. "That's the last place he'd be."

"I thought you two had a plan?"

"We did. We were going to go get his stuff from the house, put it in storage and head down to Phoenix. But when I woke up, he was gone, and I saw the paper opened to this." Michael held up the article about the Silicon Suicide. "No note, nothing."

"What are you going to do?" Roberta looked around the kitchen area.

"I hate this but I have to get that Aurora back. I think Tim's on his own now."

"Didn't you guys say something about him disappearing. What happened with that?"

Michael had no desire to involve retired CIA agents, and he wasn't under any direct orders to have Michael disappear. The Auld Alliance, the CIA cover operation, had been closed for the day, it was completely possible Tim freaked out and contacted them. Michael rubbed his eyes. "It's possible. But then there is another problem. I don't have the Aurora. Tim hid it and I don't even know where it is. He may have hid it at the house."

"Maybe that's a good thing." Roberta nodded at the article.

"I have to get it back. It's not an option. I just can't believe Tim would hang me out to dry. I knew he was nervous, but I didn't think he'd bolt like this. We've been on this operation together for a year. But there's another reason he wouldn't go to the CIA agents." Michael took a deep breath unsure of his next words. "You know Sally Thompson, Annie's friend?"

Roberta nodded.

"They are her parents."

Roberta took a moment to weigh this. "Is Sally involved?" She looked around for a place to sit, but thought better of it.

"No, definitely not. Did you know about the parents?"

"I guess I did, something Keeling said maybe. I can't remember exactly. But if Sally's not involved, that's all I need to know. So Tim's on his own, huh?"

"Look, it was his choice. We had a plan." Michael trailed off lost in thought.

"Well, I'll keep an eye out for you." Roberta turned toward the door.

"That's great. Thank you. But look, I need to get into the house and I know you are friends with Annie. I just need to look around."

Roberta stopped him by putting her hand up. "Don't even think about it. You are the F-B-I, get a warrant. And don't bring that murder and mayhem to my island. Get whatever toy you kids are fighting over and leave. I'm not Keeling and I'm not your informant, *got that*?"

"Yes, ma'am."

Roberta opened the door and left mumbling something about, "I got enough problems with the retirees on this…"

Sally pulled the car up to the last stop light before turning onto Saint Charles Place and finally going into her new home. No houseguests, no Grandma, no Annie, just she and Lorna. They'll make dinner, play with the cats, discuss the day's events, and with any luck fall asleep in each other's arms. She played out the scenario cheerfully in her mind as she parked the car in the garage.

Lorna met her at the front door. "Hello."

Sally new immediately something was very wrong. "Now what?" Sally asked. Lorna's sky blue eyes had turned a dark blue steel color, the skin on her neck had a red blotch over to one side, and the muscles in her face were drew into a tight smile. Sally froze, her eyes darting around the house from the entrance. "What's wrong?"

"Nothing. We have guests." Lorna said through her teeth.

Sally followed Lorna into the kitchen and froze in horror.

"Surprise!" Eunice and Wallace said in unison. They embraced Sally around the neck and shoulders.

Sally pulled away from them, her eyes stared at the floor. "Get out."

"Oh Sweetheart, you don't mean that." Eunice pleaded.

"Get. Out." Sally pointed toward the door.

"Now look Sally," Wallace started. "You need to listen to us."

Lorna leaned against the kitchen sink and watched with detached curiosity.

"No I don't. Please leave." Sally's eyes darted around the room but never settled on one spot. She walked out of the kitchen. Wallace and Eunice followed.

Lorna quietly walked out of the kitchen, opened the hall closet, and grabbed her coat and shoes as Wallace and

Eunice spoke over one another. Remembering her wallet she went back through the kitchen, pulled it from her purse, and left through the kitchen door.

Karen, finally, finished cutting through the extraneous paperwork and clutter from her desks' in-tray and was tidying up her as Donny came in and sat down.

"How'd it go up there?" He asked her, referring to Karen's meeting with their division chief.

She clicked off her desk lamp, shrugged, and leaned back in her chair.

"You heard about Hodge though?"

"I did." Karen shook her head. "You've got to let it go, man. I added what I could to your report and presented it to him. We have to wait and hear back. We'll get our walking orders. Did Todd have any luck tracing that burner?"

"No."

"Well, in the meantime, you might want to keep an eye out for any word on Spectorgies."

Donny tilted his head and narrowed his eyes. "You didn't hear?"

"What?"

"Jones didn't put it in?"

She raised an impatient eyebrow.

"Spectorgies put out feelers for bids to a select few customers."

Karen waited for more.

"For the Aurora. But then nothing happened."

"When?"

"Calls went out on Friday for bids today, then nothing. We don't know anything more. How could they not tell you? I mean we talked about it."

Karen smiled and shook her head. "It's okay. Jones broke the chain of command. He jumped me and went to the division head. He thinks he's being slick, going above my head and withholding information from me. But it looks bad for him, jumping protocol like that, really bad. When did you find this out?"

"Like, mid-morning, we were talking about it in the pit."

Karen laughed in contempt. "That cubicle pit is the bane of my existence. The very essence of intelligence gathering is in the craft and field work, how are you supposed to teach that in front of a computer?" She sighed and explained further, "Anyway, so, I send my report up, Chief gets it this morning, sets up a meeting with me for this afternoon. Dumb ass then jumps command and sends his report straight to the Chief, probably putting his own analysis in there with your information he gleaned from the pit."

Donny nodded. "I should have kept my mouth shut. I'm sorry about that."

"Don't worry about it."

Karen's office door flew open and they both looked up as the Chief strode in followed by Jones. "Karen, good. Donny, you're here too, good. Look, I think Jones may have a better handle on what we're dealing with in the Spectorgies operations. Let's give him a chance to take the lead on this. Anything more you find out, put it through Jones. We're going to be doing an inter-agency thing with the FBI and Homeland on this and he's better suited to represent us in that effort. Okay? Alright."

Jones stood at the doorway with an authoritatively smug look on his face.

The Chief left Karen's office, calling back to Jones. "Come on Jones, one more stop."

Donny's mouth fell open. "Even *I'm* senior to him."

Karen took it lightly, it wasn't the final nail in the coffin for her career, it was a final tap into the final nail on the coffin. "Oh, what the hell do I know? I only have twenty years service. Do whatever you want Donny."

Donny got up and left in a huff. He couldn't believe what he just saw. For the first time ever, he felt like maybe working for the NSA may not be the right job for him.

Lorna scurried across the street to Annie's house and knocked.

Annie flung open the door. "Well?"

"Go for a walk?" Lorna asked.

"Sure." Annie stepped outside.

Lorna stopped her. "You'll need a jacket and shoes."

"Oh." Annie stepped back in and reappeared instantly with a windbreaker and brown loafers on.

They walked down the block. "Well, what happened?" Annie was dying to know as they turned the corner.

Lorna opened her mouth but was speechless for a moment. "I don't know. Those people, her parents, are crazy. Like, they were saying crazy shit. Dude."

"So they *are* her parents?"

"Yeah. Sally walked in and said, 'Get out.' Who else would you have the nerve to talk to like that?"

The spring night air still had a nip to it and Annie pulled her jacket tightly around her chest.

"I can't wrap my mind around this." Lorna said.

"Sure, it's a shock, tell me what they said."

"Just that they were retiring here on the island to be close to Sally." Lorna skipped the part about the mercenary accusation Wallace had hurled about Tim and Annie.

"Even though she obviously doesn't want them."

"Obviously. But, like, okay." Lorna started and stopped, she couldn't form the words she needed to express her disbelief.

"Maybe they had come back to see her Grandma. Then decided to stay. Why does she dislike them so much that she would but such a barrier between them?"

"I guess they weren't around too much when she was growing up. Maybe they're drunks. I don't know."

"So did you just leave?"

"Yeah. Hang on." Lorna walked them into Mr. Dhaliwal's corner store.

Mr. Dhaliwal was out for the night, which was unusual but not enough for Lorna to take notice.

"Where's Mr. Dhaliwal?" Annie asked.

The man behind the counter answered briskly. "Night off. What can I get you?"

"Gimme a pack of smokes and some matches." Lorna matched his curt manner.

"You don't smoke." Annie said to Lorna.

"Neither do you." Lorna answered.

The man turned around and grabbed a pack of cigarettes and held it out to Lorna. She shrugged her consent and laid money on the counter.

Annie walked outside ahead of Lorna.

"Not for nothing, but that's kind of an expensive habit to get into." She said as Lorna came out fumbling with the wrapper.

Lorna made her first attempt to light a cigarette.

"You're supposed to inhale." She reminded Lorna.

"I know how to smoke Annie, I went to college." Lorna teased her lightly and smiled. "Here you try."

"Okay. I will." Annie said defiantly. A little frivolity might be good for her.

They both gagged and coughed out the smoke they inhaled. Annie threw her cigarette into the street. "Oh, that's gross. I can't do it."

"Hey, you just threw away," Lorna paused. "Like fifty cents."

"So? You're breathing fifty cents. You might as well swallow two quarters"

They continued walking as Lorna puffed on the cigarette. "I'm mad at Sally."

"I bet you are." Annie agreed wholeheartedly.

"Not because she *lied* about having crazy parents, but because she didn't lie about having crazy parent's, I mean, she's met my crazy family."

"But we both heard them, she didn't have a choice. Did you ever get any indication from that Grandma, remember when you visited?"

"No. Nothing. And the problem is, what else has she lied about if she lied about something so basic." Lorna thought about the thing they had said about Sally in the CIA.

"Okay, don't get mad at me but I'm going to say something here." Annie stopped and stood in front of Lorna. "Don't escalate this, just, don't turn this into something it's not."

"I feel dizzy." Lorna said.

"Give me that." Annie grabbed the cigarette from Lorna's hand and threw it into the street. "Try to think of this from Sally's point of view. Her parents, who dumped her at her grandma's to be raised, fake their deaths, and then just randomly show up. Meanwhile, Sally has had to carve out a life for herself under this shadow. She's finally happy, she's got a home, a family and then boom – Eunice and Wallace show back up. Just in time for her to have to care for them in their old age. I don't blame her for throwing them out."

"She doesn't want us here. Let's just say what we came to say and go." Wallace said from the entryway.

"Sally, darling, your friends have stolen a piece of equipment from a government contractor and they want it back."

"That has nothing to do with me."

"Oh, but it does. You don't think you'll be in the direct line of fire, once they figure out who you are?"

"Who are they?" Sally engaged with Eunice.

"Well, so far we know about two defense contractors and the NSA are involved. It's only a matter of time before the FBI and the CIA are alerted – and local law enforcement, maybe. These are forces you can't fight. You have to know when to retreat."

Sally knitted her brows together. "First of all, I have no idea what you are talking about. Secondly, I don't know what you think I know, but I don't. So whatever errand you're running for whomever in the agencies, tell them I have no involvement in it."

"Yeah, that'll work." Wallace mumbled. "Don't forget about the mercenary."

Sally turned on him, "Is that your message? Stolen merchandise, Intelligence Agencies and you threw in a mercenary now for good measure, nice touch. Got it. Message received. Are you done? 'Cause I'd like you to leave now."

Eunice relented. "Okay. If that's what you want. But we're just a phone call away now." Eunice pulled a matchbook from her purse and set it on the coffee table.

Wallace opened the front door and waited. "Remember your training. We'll be in touch." He said to Sally as Eunice walked past him and out the door.

Patience and Fortitude walked into the entryway in unison and sat down. Sally looked down at them. Patience let out a long wale and they swished their tales back and forth accusingly, Sally thought. "Oh come on, not you guys too." She pleaded.

Karen sat alone in her car staring into the depths of the parking garage. It's not the system that's messed up; it's the people in the system. How many agents had she seen buzz by her on the company ladder? How many had taken the high paying security jobs in the private sector? How many had left altogether with mysterious wads of money, boats, vacation homes or made their own retirement? But not her, she had stupidly toed the line. Now it was time for her to take her payday. She would never be this close to thirty million dollars again. Or she could take retirement; she'll soon have twenty years in the federal system and could live comfortably. She gave a cynical snort. She hated Jones and all of those, just like him, that came before.

Jones had no idea what he was doing, a fact that would benefit her in the end. She had read his analysis in the Aurora file. Not only did he not have all the players and their roles in the affair listed correctly, which would allow her to move around undetected. But he also missed the key fact that in The Hayward had only just recently hired an ex-CIA man for their security. A ex-CIA man known to Karen, a man who knew nothing about IT and everything about killing.

"'I think Jones may have a better handle on what we're dealing with'", Karen said aloud and gave a mocking laugh. "Oh sure, absolutely. He's a prodigy, that one." She started her car finally. "By the time I'm finished with him, he'll be head of the agency."

Karen backed out of the parking space and turned right instead of left out of the parking garage. She had a long night ahead of her. She had aliases to turn out, bank accounts to set up, safe houses to acquire. She needed to set up a base on Ohlone Island. The only question left would be how much coercion would it take to get Sally on board.

Annie turned her back to the wind that was hitting her in the face as they continued to stroll down the sidewalk. Lorna finally said, "You're right. I know you're right. I'm going to try to be gracious about this. But you see my point of view, don't you?"

"Of course I do. She didn't trust you enough with her past. That's a shaky foundation to build a relationship. Our partner's should be people we trust beyond all others and yet look, Tim's leaving me, and Sally turns out, doesn't trust you. Aren't we a pair?"

Lorna chuckled.

Annie thought for a minute. "You know what keeps running through my mind? Sally's parents said they had gotten involved with some security matter overseas. What does that mean? It had to be a really big deal, enough that the government would help them with new identities, like a witness protection thing."

"Yeah. I was still reeling from the shock I suppose. It's just so fucked up, you know, I thought Sally and I had kinda this common bond of losing a parent, or in her case both, and it was all a lie. She didn't *lose* her parents. She kicked them out or something. It's two totally different realities."

Lorna suppressed the urge to tell Annie everything Wallace and Eunice had said to her, especially that weird thing about the mercenary. But she needed to wait and find out what Sally had to say about it. Or did she? She definitely needed to hear Sally's side of this but, shit, how could she trust her now?

They turned another corner that put them back on Saint Charles Place. "You're right, I'm not going to escalate this. But I'm going to give myself some cooling off time." She smiled at Annie. "I can't promise anything after that."

"Ready to go back in? I'm sure Sally's in there freaking out." Annie nodded toward Lorna's house.

"Forgive me for lacking the proper empathy for her. I'll see you tomorrow. Thanks for the walk."

"No problem. Thanks for packing my husbands shit up."

"Oh." Lorna remembered. "Do you want me there in the morning when he comes by?"

"No, I'll handle it. But thanks. Come by later though."

"Will do." Lorna said, giving a little wave over her shoulder as she went up the path to the side kitchen door.

Lorna walked back in the way she left and locked the kitchen door behind her. Sally came in to the kitchen, looking pale faced and bug eyed.

"Please give me a chance to explain." Sally pleaded.

Lorna made her way over to the teakettle and filled it with water. "You have had years upon years to take that chance to explain. But only now that you have been caught in a horribly humiliating scenario you choose to tell the truth? Or have you found Jesus suddenly?"

Sally stood listening intently, waiting for Lorna's outrage fuse to ignite. But Lorna never raised her voice or spewed forth a diatribe of foul-mouthed justice. This, Sally realized, is the glowing burn of Lorna's antipathy.

"Maybe I don't want an explanation. Where are my boys?" Lorna looked at her with cold eyes.

"Sleeping, in your office." Sally offered. She really needed to find out just how much Annie had learned from Eunice and Wallace. But right now was probably not the time.

Lorna continued making herself a cup of tea, ignoring Sally's stare. Finally, Sally spoke softly. "I've worked my whole adult life to put them and my past behind me. I never told you because I don't want them in what I've built for myself, what we have – I don't want them to take it away."

Lorna put three butter cookies on the saucer with her tea and paused as she walked past Sally. "Then you should have trusted me. They can't take something away that I don't even have. No matter what you *meant* to do, *I've* been completely humiliated to your family and my family and our friends. I'm the one who looks like she can't be trusted." Lorna walked back into her office and shut the door behind her.

Sally thought fast. If she could keep Lorna talking to her, then she had a chance. She knocked softly on the door before opening it. Lorna was petting Fortitude, who was perched on the catwalk. "Look I don't know what they told you but I doubt it has any resemblance to *my* truth. They probably regaled you with their nail biting, yet somehow hysterical, experiences in the CIA. You don't have to trust me, but whatever else you do, don't trust them." Sally started to close the door but thought better of it and reopened it, "I was only twenty three when they tried to recruit me, ya' know."

To Sally's relief Lorna sat down at her desk and looked up to her. "Close the door please." Lorna said calmly.

But she couldn't do it, she couldn't leave, and she couldn't click over to the survival mode as she had with Tessa. She stood dumb and frozen in time. Lorna got up and slowly closed the door in her face.

CHAPTER 10

RUMOR IS TRUTH, IN DRAG

There had long been a rumor swirling around the San Francisco HUD offices that caused the employees to be extra careful not to call their boss a pud sucker or use any threatening language over the office phone lines. Sally thought briefly about this before she called Tessa from her office phone. If a rumor is repeated enough, it becomes common knowledge. Sometimes common knowledge will become a fact, especially if the rumor did not spark enough outrage that caused a backlash that would squash the rumor. Whether or not it was true, Sally couldn't care less. And at this point, she actually hoped someone was listening. Her nightmare had happened and Sally was now unfettered. What are they going to do, fire her for going through CIA training? Reaching out to Tessa was not a calculated maneuver. She genuinely needed to talk to someone about this.

"That's about the worst case scenario right there." Tessa said after Sally explained last night's fiasco to her. "How did she seem when you left her?"

"That's why I'm so worried Tessa. She was so quiet, so relaxed. There was no screaming. I've never seen her like that."

"That's how she gets. One time when she was young, and I don't know what had happened but I was really mad at her, so I told her little friends that she had head lice. She didn't scream or throw a fit. It was like she just went dead inside."

"Yes! That's exactly how she reacted. What happened?"

"I ended up having to shave off all my hair because somehow I ended up with head lice. Then, of course, this boy I had been going out with stop calling me. This was after Dad had laid into me for spreading such a socially damaging lie about Lorna around. It took her a month to even say excuse me when she body checked me in the hallway. By this point I had lost all my sight so needless to say it was a *very* uncomfortable three or four months. She'd sit in a room and not make a sound, just watching me."

"That's cruel."

"Yes. But I never did it again."

"I don't know what to do."

"Honestly, I didn't think she'd take your news like this. I thought she'd be mad as a wet hen but then think it was cool, somehow. It's not like she can stay mad forever. Give her some cooling off time, if she won't speak to you maybe you can explain in a letter or something."

"I always thought she'd try to get me to teach her, like, Moscow rules or something."

"Oh! Quill and I thought the same thing. We were worried she'd be mad but start writing everything in lemon juice or something."

"Do you think I should get a hotel room for a week or so?"

"No. That's too far. Just respect her space, let her come around to it."

"You think she will?"

"Oh Sally, I don't know. I wish I could give you comfort and tell you everything was going to be okay, that she'll forgive you but I can't. I want to. But you know that's up to Lorna."

Sally leaned back in her chair and looked up at the fluorescent lights. "So the best I can hope for is a bad four months."

"I'm thinkin'." Tessa confirmed.

"Okay, well, okay. I can do four months."

"What is she doing today?" Tessa asked.

"I don't know, probably helping Annie again."

"Did your parents give you any indication that they were still working?"

"They had a story, of course, but I think it's most likely just a story, a way to get a toe hold in my life."

"It's weird though, the timing of it."

"When it rains, it pours, that's for sure."

"Well look, we never talked, okay?" Tessa offered.

Sally agreed, "I haven't talked to you since I took you to the airport."

They both hung up, leaving Sally staring at her paperwork. What the hell else could possibly happen?

Lorna stood in the doorway of Annie's office. "You're going to have to help me go through that wall of media you got down there." Lorna was saying, referring to the living room bookshelves that stretched across the whole wall.

"I know. I'm almost done here."

"Really? Like all caught up?"

"Yes. And I'm going to be ready for the out of office meeting. Heather St. James be damned."

"Ew. We hate Heather St. James. Okay, I'll wait downstairs."

Lorna went downstairs to wait and made herself an iced tea in the kitchen when the opened door to the cellar caught her eye. Another difference between her and Annie's craftsman style houses was that Annie's house had a cellar. Lorna crept up to it and smacked the door shut, that cellar always creeps her out.

Annie walked into the kitchen. "You know what I want to do?"

"Get rip roaring drunk?" Lorna asked hopefully.

"Yes! That is exactly what I want to do. Blow off some steam!"

"Tie one on, get smashed, inebriated, destroy some brain cells?"

"Three sheets to the wind."

"Blown out of my shorts!"

Annie winked. "That is a well thought out plan."

"Should we invite the Queen of England?" Lorna asked about their 80-something year old neighbor, Mrs. Strangler.

"Oh I don't know. Every time we drink with her, somehow, the cops show up."

Lorna laughed. "I know! She's awesome."

Mrs. Strangler, who had to be 80 something years old, which was a guesstimate between Annie and Lorna, was without fail, impeccably mannered. She dressed tastefully in the fashionable 1950's era, with the ever-present purse dangling from her forearm. Mrs. Strangler also had a "hollow leg" and a gambling addiction. Every Friday night for as long as anyone could remember Mrs. Strangler had poker night. The other five people who were lucky enough to get invites from her ranged from the mayor in office, to catholic priests, to the kid down the street, to the occasional business tycoon. All of who would not dare turn down the invite. When the Queen of England summoned you, you arrived on time, and with your pockets filled with cash.

"I don't know, let's go to karaoke!"

"YES, I feel a deep need to be a fool with other fools. Perfect."

"It's a deal, now let's tackle that wall."

Tim sat on the rickety stairs that led to the cellar listening to Annie and Lorna make their plans. Hopefully, they'll finish the packing before they go. Something must have happened with Lorna and Sally too, he thought. As annoying as he found Lorna could be, right now he felt nothing but gratitude for her. Not just for being a good friend to Annie and packing up his stuff but also for getting Annie out of the house for a little while tonight. As soon as they leave, he thought, he'll contact Michael from the house phone. They can load what he needs in the surveillace van he had stashed over at the old military base and they can head to Phoenix.

Sally walked to the corner of 1st Street to catch the O line bus home. She had spent the better part of the day worrying about something she couldn't control, which frustrated her further. Maybe she should have asked Tessa to send a message to her contact in the CIA about that mercenary thing her parents had mentioned. No, it was important she play this straight, keep her head down and walk the line. Lorna had every right to be mad at her. She had chosen to not say anything about a very significant part of her life, but she hadn't lied. Except about the parents part. If she really wanted to be manipulative she'd invite them to dinner and then she wouldn't have anything further to explain to Lorna. Sally smiled to herself. Her grin melted as the other shoe dropped. She looked into a once familiar face.

"Got a minute?" Karen asked her.

"Nope." Sally looked around for an escape.

Karen quickly flashed her DOJ badge. "Come on, for old time's sake."

"Please go away." Sally's face flushed with confusion and rage.

"I just need you to listen. Five minutes." Karen checked her watch. "We have time."

"Fuck. You."

"We can do this the hard way if you want." Karen offered sardonically. "Now that doesn't sound like the Sally Soucek I know."

"You don't know me, Nurse."

Karen smiled. "I haven't been called that in *years*. God, we were so young."

Sally glared at her.

"I'm with the NSA now." Karen kept her voice low and casual. "I'm heading up an inter-agency team with the FBI and the NRO. But I need some informants. Nothing too deep, just some eyes and ears over there on Ohlone Island and the East Bay."

Sally slowly shook her head.

"Listen, free money for nothing. No strings attached. Truly. Just take my card then."

Sally did not think it was a coincidence that Nurse and her parents have shown up at the same. "It's just old home week, huh?"

Nurse nodded smiling. "Sure."

Annie did not believe that the two pitchers of beer she and Lorna drank at the trivia night in McDuff's Pub had anything to do with how light and graceful she felt at this moment. It had nothing to do with the fact that Tim did not show up to sign the divorce papers and pick up his shit from the house today. It had nothing to do with the fact that Sally has turned out to be a big fat lying liar. It had everything to do with her deep and abiding friendship with Lorna who stumbled a few feet behind her as they made their way home from the pub, and the very awesome fact that they won the music trivia night. 'Cause *in fact* they were the superstars of the rockin' trivia night! Did she say that aloud?

"If I were music." Annie announced to a streetlamp. "I'd be jazz."

Lorna fell in step with Annie. "If you were music, you'd be a dirge. If I were music, I'd be the pledge of allegiance!"

"No, that doesn't make sense." Annie protested.

"But people would be forced to say me everyday." Lorna was triumphant in her pronouncement.

"But it's not music. No, you'd be some random infomercial tune that gets stuck in the head and makes people crazy. Then they'd start humming it spreading it around like a virus."

"But I'd be viral!" Lorna collided into Annie. "This is our street."

"Oh. Right. I cannot wait to pass out. I'm not even going to wash my face."

"Rebel!" Lorna pointed at Annie.

"Wanna stay in our guestroom?" Annie offered.

"No. I'm going to stand my ground. Or lie, lay on my ground. I mean my bed."

"Good for you, sister." Annie belched. "Excuse me."

Lorna crossed over to her side of the street. "Till the morrow, good tidings, and all that shit."

Sally could hear Lorna stumble up the porch stairs and come inside. She had already eaten dinner, cleaned up the kitchen, and made up the guest bedroom for herself. And now she slid between the sheets, listening to Lorna meander and stumble up the stairs. She switched off the bedside light and glanced at the clock, which read: 11:45. She made sure the alarm was switched on and closed her eyes. She knew Lorna was drunk. She thought about going to get her off the stairs but then thought better of it. Give Lorna the space she needs would be her new mantra. Make room for forgiveness.

There was a crazy bird screeching outside that seemed to be getting closer. Sally sat up in bed. What was that? She heard Lorna stumble down the stairs and the front door open. It was Annie and she sounded frantic. Sally jumped up from the bed and ran downstairs where she found Annie crumbled on the floor and covered in blood.

"911! 911! It's Tim! It's Tim!" Annie tripped and collapsed in a bloody heap on the floor.

Lorna grabbed her cell phone off the shelf and focused her eyes on the keypad and speed dialed a number.

"My name is Lorna Tollison. I live at 65 Saint Charles Place." Lorna was overly enunciating each word as she spoke. "I don't know, there's a lot of blood. You need to send an ambulance and the police to 68 Saint Charles Place, immediately."

Sally took off across the street. Annie's front door was still swinging open when she walked in. At first she looked around cautiously from the door and then took a few tentative steps inside just past entryway. She looked into the living room. Tim's dead body lay in a pond of blood. The deep red gash across his neck was gaping open. The sight took Sally's breath away. She stood fighting the urge to do *something*. No, this is a crime scene. Lorna came bounding up behind her. She bumped into her back and pushed to get through. Sally turned and forced Lorna back. "No. Lorna, no."

Lorna looked at Tim's body. "Oh my God!"

Annie came right up behind Lorna. "Do something! Help him! He needs help!" She kept repeating, trying to fight her way past Lorna and Sally.

"No. Annie. Stop. It's too late!" Lorna held Annie back.

Annie inhaled in a violent tremor and passed out.

Sally caught her mid-fall. "Help me get her back to our place. Are the police coming?" She asked Lorna.

"Yes." Lorna put her shoulder under Annie's right arm, Sally took the left and they dragged Annie back to their house and laid her on the couch.

Mrs. Strangler walked in still wearing her nightgown and robe. "What on earth is going on?"

"Mrs. Strangler, something horrible happened and the police are on their way. Annie needs your help can you stay here with her?" Sally asked.

"What happened?" Mrs. Strangler demanded.

"Tim is dead. He's in their house. We need to go back."

"Okay." Mrs. Strangler looked down at the blood all over Annie.

Lorna and Sally walked back to Annie's house. "Did you see anyone?" Lorna asked.

"No, the place was dark when I came home on the bus. Was Annie expecting him home?"

"This morning he was supposed to be here but he never showed up."

"What time did you guys leave for the bar?"

"Like around eight."

"Look, give the police a general idea of what happened. Then lawyer up, don't let them question Annie. I'm going to call a someone to represent Annie."

"Why? We don't know anything." Lorna asked.

"Because you're drunk and because you and Annie are going to be the prime suspects."

Sally carefully walked over and felt Tim's wrist. It wasn't particularly warm but the body wasn't stiff yet. She carefully retraced her steps to the door. "Stay here and send the EMT's over to our house, make sure they take Annie to the hospital." Sally left again and went back across the street.

Lorna looked around the room. She didn't know what to do. She pulled her cell phone out of her front jeans pocket and snapped a picture of Tim's body. She stepped back and took a picture of the room as the ambulance pulled up.

Two EMT's, a man and a woman hurried up the walk. "What happened?" The man asked.

Lorna pointed to Tim's body. They pushed passed her and felt for a pulse.

Lorna looked over and saw a police cruiser pull up. After a few moments, a young policeman got out and came to the door.

"What happened?" He asked Lorna.

Lorna pointed to the living room where the male EMT was talking on a cell phone.

"What happened?" He asked Lorna again.

"I don't know."

"Have you been drinking?"

"Yes, I have."

"Do you live here?"

"No. I don't."

"Stay here." He ordered Lorna.

Lorna nodded and mumbled, "Okay." As he walked back out to his cruiser and got in.

The female EMT came over to her. "Did you find him like this?"

"Yes."

"How long ago?"

"About two minutes before I called you guys. So maybe fifteen minutes ago. What time is it?"

"It's midnight. Look, we have to call CSI and the coroner. Do you have anyone you can call?"

"No, I'm good. But his wife is across the street in my house, she needs to get to a hospital, she passed out. We have a neighbor with her now."

The EMT looked across the street. "With the front lights on?"

"Yeah, just go on in."

"Kyle." The female EMT got the attention of her partner. "We've got another one across the street."

Kyle and the female EMT passed the police officer on the front stairs.

"Can you step outside ma'am?"

Lorna followed him out to the sidewalk where the neighbors were starting to come out to their lawns. He flashed his flashlight beam in her face. "What's your name?"

"Lorna Tollison." She put her hand in front of the light. "Do you mind?"

"Put your hand down Ms. Tollison."

Lorna heard another man's voice from behind her. "She lives in that house with that other woman."

Lorna swung around. "Who the hell are *you*?" She turned back to the policeman. "I would appreciate it if you'd stop flashing that light in my eyes first."

"Put your hands behind your head please."

Lorna took a deep breath and did as he asked.

"Get down on your knees."

Again, she did as he asked.

He put the plastic handcuffs on her, led her to the back of his patrol car, put her in, and shut the door. Just then another set of lights pulled up and another unmarked police cruiser pulled up behind the car she was in. The fire department showed up and men and women were streaming in and out of Annie's house to get a look. She panned around the scene unfolding and sighed. She giggled and bowed her head down. "It's like the Marx Brother's out there. 'Gentlemen, I've *had a* wonderful night, but this wasn't it.'"

At one point, Lorna tried to wish herself sober but the alcohol was coursing through her veins. She lifted her head back up and tried to focus her eyes. Sally was in an animated conversation with the police. "Oh, this should be good." A white truck pulled up ahead and blocked the street, the tailgate read: Ohlone CSI. Lorna watched as Sally led the police to the house and back to the sidewalk. Finally, the young officer opened the car door again.

"Come on." He waggled a finger at her.

Lorna watched as Sally kept talking to the plain-clothes policeman and leaned her head back as he snapped off the cuffs. "What's wrong boy, mommy don't let you cuff her to the bed anymore?" She muttered at him.

The young police officer walked over next to what Lorna assumed was the detective in charge and scowled at her. The EMT's were carrying Annie out on a stretcher with an oxygen mask on her face. Mrs. Strangler walked with them. Lorna hurried over to them as they were loading Annie into the back of the ambulance.

"Will you stay with her for a while and I'll come relieve you as soon as I can?"

"Yes, of course." Mrs. Strangler nodded.

Lorna realized Mrs. Strangler was still in her nightgown and robe and didn't even have her proverbial purse hanging off her arm as the EMT helped her into the truck. She walked back over to Sally and the detective.

"…witnesses after the fact." Sally was saying. "Unless you're going to be bringing us in for formal questioning in relation to this murder, in which case we'll want our attorney's present, then it can wait until tomorrow. I'm sure you have your hands full right now."

"Tonight would be better." He countered.

"That's fine then, however, we'll be making a formal complaint for false arrest, false imprisonment, and police brutality. Lorna let me see your wrists."

Lorna held out her arms.

"I think I'll have plenty of witnesses. We'll want to get some pictures of that. Go inside." She ordered Lorna.

Lorna said nothing but walked inside their house and left Sally to do her law thing out there. She shut the front door behind her and went straight for the kitchen. Did Sally really want her to take pictures of her arms? She looked down at her wrists. They were a little red, but not bad. She needed to sober up. She needed to eat some bread. She opened a loaf of bread and started cramming slices into her mouth washing them down with water.

It could have been the fright of hearing the door slam or the amount of bread she crammed down her gullet. The minute she lifted her head off the kitchen table Lorna felt her stomach contract and barely made it to the sink before puking up bread and beer. Someone turned the water on and she felt a cool rag being placed on the back of her neck. Lorna leaned up to see Roberta helping her back to a chair.

"You alright?" Roberta sat across from her at the table.

"Yeah. Oh Roberta, I'm still drunk. I need to get to the hospital and relieve Mrs. Strangler."

"Not now you don't. She'll be okay for a few minutes."

"Where's Sally?"

"She's getting Annie's dog's settled in the garage. You wanna tell me what happened?"

"Yeah, um. Annie and I went out drinking tonight. Uh, first we went to karaoke at The Last Resort, and then we stopped at McDuff's for trivia when we were walking home. We got back here about – I don't know – 11:30, 11:45. I was taking my shoes off on the stairs and I heard Annie screaming. I threw open the door and she fell inside, all covered in blood. Then Sally came downstairs and ran across the street and I called the police. When I got over there, Sally was already there and Annie came running in behind me and passed out. We carried her back here."

"What time did you leave to walk up to The Last Resort?"

"About eight-ish?"

"So, was Annie expecting him home tonight?" Roberta asked.

"No, he was supposed to come this morning or early today and take his stuff, but he never showed. Sally and I had been fighting, so Annie and I just decided to go blow off some steam."

Sally came in and sat down at the table. "Does Annie have a dog walker?"

"Yes. It's, hang on, let me think. I just called her the other day." Lorna flopped her head back in thought.

Sally continued, "Well look, give the dog walker a call in the morning and set up the service for a couple of weeks."

Roberta asked, "Do you guys know Tim's family? Someone should give them a call."

"It's just Tim's mom and step-dad in San Jose and a brother out in Hawaii. Annie said they had really given her the cold shoulder since this divorce thing. Is it wrong to give Annie a few more hours before they come swooping in? Is that wrong?"

Sally and Roberta grimaced and shrugged at her.

"It's just that I think the last thing she needs right now are suspicious minds or have them whispering in that detectives ear. Roberta, she couldn't have done it, she was with me – or she couldn't have had it done for her. You *know* Annie."

"I know." Roberta scanned their eyes and dropped her voice to an almost whisper, "That's the new homicide detective I was telling you about the other day and you better believe he's going to be looking to make his mark in the department with this, I'm sure."

"So okay, we give it at least until tonight. But, I mean, what do we do now?" Lorna pointed her question to Roberta.

"Do you know if Tim left a will?" Roberta asked.

Lorna and Sally shook their heads, no.

Roberta pulled out a notebook from her pocket. "I generally tell people to go to this website. They have a checklist of things to do." She wrote something down on the pad and tore off the sheet for Lorna. "I can't imagine the coroner holding the body too long. Do as much as you can now, because once this adrenaline wears off, you're going to be a mess." She looked over at Sally. "Now you, what can you tell me?"

Sally shook her head regretfully. "I got off the bus about eight forty-five. I had to work late and you know, I didn't see their lights on over there. I checked because I thought Lorna might still be there. Then I came in and made myself something to eat, cleaned the kitchen, and went upstairs. I was in bed about nine-thirty or ten and woke up again when Lorna got home, it was exactly eleven forty-five because I looked over at the clock."

"So it had to have happened between eight and eleven thirty." Lorna nodded to herself. "Mrs. Strangler is at the hospital with Annie right now. I told her I'd come relieve her."

"I'll go." Sally offered. "Can you work on the list and maybe you'd like a shower. I'll run over to the hospital, check on Annie, and bring Mrs. Strangler back."

"They've probably sedated Annie, if she's in for overnight observation." Roberta offered.

"You'll go first thing, well," Sally glanced over at the clock, which read: 2:12, "in a few hours."

"That house is going to be a crime scene for a couple of days." Roberta nodded. "Can you bring Annie back here?"

"Of course." Sally said. "But we have to make our statements to the detective tomorrow. I'll have Chris set up the appointment, sorry, we had to lawyer up."

Roberta nodded her consent.

"And we're going to be filing charges against that patrolman who cuffed Lorna."

Roberta shook her head. "Yeah. I don't know, do what you gotta do. I hate to hear it though." Roberta turned to Lorna expectantly.

Lorna nodded. "He didn't have to do that. I know I smell like a distillery, but I was answering his questions just like I am with you now."

Roberta shrugged and stood up. "Yeah. I'm sorry that happened to you."

Sally walked Roberta to the front door and returned to the kitchen. "Go upstairs and lay down. There's nothing anyone can do right now. Okay?"

"I never thought being drunk could be so horrible. Lorna said drearily. "This has got to be some kind of nightmare."

"No, unfortunately not. Come upstairs, come on, I'll help you." Sally helped Lorna up. Walking up the stairs she realized nothing will ever be the same for them on their little island.

CHAPTER 11

THE INVISIBLE LINK

Lorna jolted awake with an abrupt gasp, and looked around her bedroom. She inhaled a shallow breath and grabbed her forehead with both hands. She needed to get to the hospital, but first, she thought, she'll have to shave her tongue.

The shower revived her. She put her clothes on carefully and went downstairs. Sally had left a note on the kitchen table: *Went into the city to grab some work. Be back as soon as I can. Annie is okay at the hospital. Call me when you wake up.* Lorna opened the refrigerator and grabbed the orange juice out.

She sat down at the table, tipped up the juice carton, and drank the rest of the orange juice down. Her hand came down no the table with a smack. Remembering the Groucho Marx line in the back of the police cruiser horrified her. She tried to focus on what had been different lately. What could have led up to this? Is it even remotely possible that Annie could have had *anything* to do with this? Images of Tim covered in his own blood flashed through her mind. Is there anyway that detective could try to hang this on Annie? No, she thought, it's just not possible. She'd been with Annie almost consistently since last Friday, for five days. Then, there's this thing with Sally. What was it Wallace had said about a mercenary? She shook her head. No, that can't be right, they were absolutely delusional. But still, she felt like needed to talk to someone. She went over to the kitchen phone and called Tessa.

"Hey."

"Hey. It's me."

"What's wrong?"

"Tim was murdered last night."

"Holy shit! Did they catch who did it? I mean how? Where?"

"Tim was supposed to come get his stuff but didn't show up so Annie and I went out for drinks. When we got back, Annie found him dead in their living room. His throat had been slashed – like from ear to ear."

"Where is she?"

"She was sedated and taken to the hospital for observation. We were really pretty drunk when we got back, and it was a shock."

"Okay. What can I do?"

"Nothing, right now. I think we have to wait and let the police do their thing. We're going to bring her back to our house when the hospital releases her."

"That's good."

"I need to talk to you about something else too. So, Monday – I don't even know how to get into this, um, so these people showed up and they claimed to be Sally's parents."

"Lorna, just stop." Tessa spoke deliberately. "Now you know people are always making claims because they think you two are an inroad to get to me."

"What—" Lorna scowled at the phone but Tessa continued on.

"Just ignore them. I have full faith in Sally. Do you understand? Full faith. She's the best thing you have going for you right now. So have a little faith in her too."

Lorna paused and looked around the kitchen.

Tessa kept silent.

"Have you lost your fucking mind?"

"No. I'm just telling you I don't want to hear talk smack about your partner."

"You didn't even give me a chance to say anything."

"Keep it that way. Anything you have to say, say it to Sally."

"You're such a Judas, you know that? I called because I'm upset about some things, some really big shit is going on here and you shut me down. Thanks sister. You're *the best*. You know what? The next time you need help with something, call your own fucking plumbers. Do *you* understand?" Lorna slammed the phone down.

Before she was able to wipe the incredulity off her face the phone rang again.

"Hello."

"I just need you to listen to me for a minute." Quill Tollison's baritone southern drawl commanded Lorna's attention. "Everything is going to be fine." He continued thoughtfully, "If you're going to be mad at anyone, be mad at me. I've known about the parents for a while and I didn't tell you and I'm sorry. It just seemed to me that everything was being done to protect everyone else. Do you understand?"

"I think so." Lorna looked around the kitchen. Why did her father know this too?

"Good, just try to listen to what each other has to say. Okay?" He said graciously.

"Yeah."

"Now then." Quill changed subjects, "Was it a robbery?"

"We don't know anything yet." Lorna said.

"She's gonna need some help."

"I know, we're bringing her back to our place."

"No, well okay, but I mean with the funeral arrangements and the end of life care. Has his immediate family been notified?" Quill gently got down to business.

"No, not yet."

"Okay. Then let me make a couple of calls. I'll bring someone in that can handle the nuts and bolts."

"Dad. The police are going to try to pin this on her. The house is all taped up with crime scene tape and Annie's in the hospital with shock."

"Okay. Okay, one thing at a time. Does she have an attorney?"

"Yes. Sally got someone."

"Good. He or she?"

"He."

"Then *he* can handle her defense. Not you and not Sally. Understand? I'll bring someone else in to handle the arrangements. You two are going to have to be a buffer for her. You're going to have to work together."

"I know. I'm getting ready to go to the hospital now."

"We can process everything else later. How's that sound?"

"That's fine."

"It's going to be alright. Right?" He added gently.

"Right. Is Tessa there?"

"Do you want to talk to her?"

"No. Just tell her she's a fuzzy piece of shit."

Quill chuckled aloud. "Okay Darlin', I'll let her know."

"No, I'm serious," Lorna started up again.

Quill hung up the phone. Patience and Fortitude came into the kitchen and sat down next to each other and looked up at her in their uniform manner. "It's a conspiracy." She said to them.

Sally walked out of her office and down the wide hallway of San Francisco's Federal Housing Authority. She stopped at Katie's cubicle.

"Could I see you in my office for a minute?" She asked Katie.

"Uh oh." Katie looked up at Sally and pushed a couple of buttons on her phone before getting up.

Sally smiled. "It's nothing, I just want some privacy."

Katie followed Sally back to her office and shut the door behind her.

"So, I'm going to have to take a few more days off, probably the rest of the week."

"Okay, shouldn't be a problem, you've got tons of use or lose time acquired, like sixty hours or something."

"I'm going to take a lot of my case load home and work from there."

"Why don't you just take the time off? We'll shift some of your case load over."

"Because it's not fair to do that."

"What do you mean? They do it to you all the time." Katie had an edge to her voice.

"Yes, but I'm not *them*." Sally was a little taken aback that Katie didn't even ask why she was taking time off. But she decided to offer it anyway. She needed Katie's eyes and ears at the office. "Last night my partner's best friend, well our neighbor, was murdered."

Katie's head dipped down. "What?"

"Yeah. And she needs our help. Lorna and Annie, her best friend, found the body, it was bad."

"Oh my God."

"So, here's the deal. I'm a little worried about the press. And I'm a lot worried about office gossip."

"Yeah. I'll bet."

"I'm going to go in and talk to Scott. Let him know what's going on, and that I'm taking the rest of the week off, but will be available by phone. But can you do me a favor and keep your ears and eyes out for me?"

"Yeah man, they eat the weak around here."

"Exactly. I honestly just really don't need that superfluous office crap right now."

"Not a problem."

"But look, you don't have to be my office mole, ya' know? I'm not asking that."

"Sally, it's fine. I got your back. I know how to handle it."

"Thanks Katie."

Katie opened the door to let herself out. "You're welcome." She said and left.

Sally looked at Scott's phone line and buzzed over to his office.

"Yeah." He yelled.

"Got a minute?" She asked keeping her tone light and casual.

Lorna walked into Annie's hospital room. Annie looked so small under the blankets with just her head sticking out.

Lorna pulled the chair over to the bed and sat down. After a few minutes Annie stirred, Lorna stood back up as Annie opened her eyes.

"Hi."

Annie just blinked at her.

"Annie, do you know what's going on?" Lorna said carefully.

Annie nodded and turned her head away.

"Has anyone come to talk to you?"

"Roberta." Annie mumbled.

"Okay. Good. They're going to release you in a little while and we're going to take you back to our place. We have Bert and Ernie."

Annie started gently crying. She pulled the sheet up over her face as the tension contorted it.

Lorna gave her another minute before she continued softly, "Now, Mrs. Strangler has offered to sit with you at our place if you'd like. But Sally and I are going to go with the attorney and give our statements to the police. You can come if you'd like to get it over with or we can put it off a little longer."

Annie gave a mucus filled cough and wheezed out, "I want to go home."

"I know. But you can't right now, they have the police crime tape up and they're doing their investigation. You'll have to come to our house, at least for today."

Annie continued crying shaking her head from side to side. "I'm so sorry."

"No, it's okay, Sally's going to be here any minute. Do you want to put some clothes on? I brought you some sweats."

Annie rolled over to her side, facing away from Lorna. Lorna got the sweats out of the bag and laid them on the foot of the bed. The door opened and Roberta popped her head in and signaled for Lorna to come out of the room.

Lorna gently shut the door behind her and walked to the other side of the hallway, out of earshot of Annie's door.

"Dude. She's a *mess*. Like, she's going to need drugs just to function. There's no way she can make a statement, attorney or not."

"Look, I just came from the command room."

"What?"

"That's what Jim call's it, his command room." Roberta said regretfully. "You guys need to get in there and get your statements in, and I don't know, give her whatever drugs to pull it together because he's building his case. I imagine he's going to try to get it to the D.A. by tomorrow."

"With what evidence?"

"He found the divorce papers."

"Shit. From the kitchen table, Annie signed them before we left."

"And the knife that killed Tim came from the kitchen. Those boxes in the dining room had been rifled through."

"Hang on, I filled those boxes myself, they had been neatly stacked."

"Well look, something happened in there because everything had been dumped out of them. It does look like there had been a fight or something. Two against one? Then you and Annie go out drinking?"

"Why would we leave Tim there to bleed to death? This is insane."

"Well, people have had worse alibi's."

"Alibi's? What is that? It sounds to me like Tim walked in on someone trying to rob the place."

Sally walked around the corner and saw Roberta talking with Lorna. "Shit," she said under her breath.

"Is she ready?" Sally asked Lorna.

"Annie's, like," Lorna shook her head ruefully. "Dude."

"Look, I've got to get back." Roberta said.

"Thanks Roberta." Lorna nodded.

"I'm going to go get her checked out at the nurses station." Sally said.

Lorna went back in the room where Annie had buried herself under the covers.

After they settled Annie and Mrs. Strangler in at their house, Lorna and Sally met Chris, Annie's lawyer, at the police station. Chris' instructions to Lorna were simple. 'Don't speak unless spoke to. Pause before speaking. And answer, factually, the question put before you. Nothing else.' It was a lot harder than it sounded.

The detective's questions were not fill in the blank, multiple choice, or yes/no questions. The detective interrupted her a lot while she went over their movements of the night. Then would ask her to start in the middle of the story and go backwards. He'd jump ahead and ask her something about after they found the body. Then he'd skip back and ask about how Lorna had packed the boxes and why. He asked about the divorce. Which Chris would object to those questions as 'hearsay'. Then the detective would rephrase the question and Chris would jump in again.

After an hour the detective got frustrated and started the questioning all over again but in his questioning he'd changed the facts and she would have to correct him. Finally, after an hour and a half Chris had enough and stopped the interview. He warned the detective off with harassment, the detective ended the interview and clicked off the recorder. The detective pulled out a notepad and pushed it toward Lorna.

Chris reached over and pushed it back toward the detective. "You can have your typist type up the interview and my client will sign it."

Lorna wasn't sure what had just happened but she was led out of the interview room and took a seat in the front waiting area, where she thought she'd see Sally. Her heart sank as she saw Sally being led into the interview room from a different office.

Her mind wandered back to Roberta. Roberta had been so keen on getting Annie in here. But was it in Annie's best interest or was Roberta looking to stay above the fray with this new detective? But Roberta must know, in her heart, Annie could never have done this. Such a violent and gruesome act and on top of which Annie was half Tim's size. Roberta is a survivor though. She had survived a tour in Afghanistan and one in Iraq. Not to mention giving birth to three children and is now climbing through the ranks of an essentially all white boy's club in the police department. No, at her core, Roberta is a survivor and this guy was no Detective Keeling. Roberta might have to survive his ignorance and stupidity, no matter what truth is in her heart of hearts.

She suppressed the urge to find Roberta and kick her in the teeth. Now she was going to have to work on Roberta. If Roberta was being that Fat Head detectives errand girl, then Lorna would just have change tactics with Roberta. She'd have to get messages to the Fat Head detective by pulling Roberta closer into their circle.

Maybe Chris can arrange to have Annie submit a written statement until she's mentally fit for questioning. Why didn't that Fat Head ask about Tim's known associates or maybe someone with a grudge? Annie would have to go through the house to see if anything was stolen, of course. But then again, Roberta may be trying to undercut this guy and solve this case. The detective had asked about the cellar, which was odd. Lorna just now remembered the door had been ajar, at some point, and she had closed it. Had the killer been there with them? She thought hard, when was that? Holy crap. It was yesterday. Before they went out. Lorna looked around the waiting area, she needed to tell someone about that.

Lorna's thoughts were flying around in her head until she saw Sally emerge from the interview room. It felt like Sally had only been in there for five minutes but when Lorna looked at the clock she realized it had been a half hour. She stood up as Sally neared. Chris came out of the room and they waited for him to catch up.

"Come on." Chris said. And they walked outside and down the steps of the police department building. "You are not to talk with the police any further. I'm going to need Annie to write out a statement in the next couple of days, but I'll go over that with her. So, Sally we'll be in touch." The last statement was a command, Lorna noticed.

"Yes. Thank you Chris."

"Well?" Lorna asked after they got into the car.

Sally shook her head. "They don't have anything. Not one shred of evidence. He's trying to build a case out of circumstantial evidence."

"That Fat Head detective?"

"Yes." Sally was tense and completely humorless.

"Can we talk about Roberta before we get home?"

"Don't worry about Roberta. She's a good detective but keep that in mind when she randomly shows up to *share* information with you."

"Yes." Lorna realized they were thinking about the same thing, when Roberta showed up at the hospital before Sally got there.

"There's something else we need to talk about though."

Over the last few hours, Lorna had almost completely forgot about Sally's parent's showing up. The thought of having to get into all of it right now shriveled up her last bit of energy she was clinging to right now.

"That's fine. But honestly, if you want a good outcome to that, you are going to have to let me get some sleep. I'm absolutely, completely done. There's nothing left here. You know what I'm saying? I can't. Not right now."

"I know. I'm going to get a hotel room, I think, for the next couple of days."

"Oh the hell you are. You're not leaving me alone in this. This shit gets hard and you're gonna cut and run? Wow, ya' know I am learning *a lot* about you now. You're a fucking nightmare. Just take me home and go then."

"That's not what I mean." Sally's voice was even. "I'm trying to tell you I want you to get some good rest. We have some things to talk about. Do you think it's a coincidence that my parents show up and then Tim is dead?"

Lorna put her head in her hand. "Oh my God, Sally, what are you saying?"

Sally pulled the car over to the side of the road and parked it.

She turned to Lorna and pulled her hand off her face. "Look at me. You have every single right to be mad at me, not to trust me. But if you ever had a single true spark of faith in me, you've got to believe me now. There is a lot of stuff I have to tell you. I have an idea about what's going on here and I know you are exhausted. I'm exhausted, it's been a really rough few weeks."

"So you think running off to a hotel while I cater to Annie's needs is going to help me?"

"No, I just want to divert anything else from happening."

"Are people after you?"

"No. I have to assume they got what they came for."

"With who, Tim?"

"Yes."

They paused as the engine hummed. Lorna spoke first. "Okay, here's what I want. I want you to take me home. I want to get a good night's sleep. Then I want to go over all this with you. But I don't want you to leave me there alone with Annie. Not now."

"Okay. It's a deal." Sally agreed and started the car back on the road again.

When Sally got back from walking Mrs. Strangler home she went upstairs where she found Lorna crawling into bed. "Um, look," Sally sat on the edge of the bed. "I was wondering if we could have that talk tonight. We don't have to, but here's my thinking on this. The cat is already out of the bag on, well, things, once Tim's parents find out. I just feel like."

Lorna blinked at Sally struggling to get the words out.

Sally stammered onward. "I think if we can get through this—"

"Well, you've convinced me." With obvious regret, Lorna got back out of bed. "Come on, I don't want to wake Annie."

Lorna put on the kettle for tea and sat down at the kitchen table.

"First of all," Sally struggled to start, "what I mean to say, okay—"

"Hi, I'm Lorna Tollison, I'm a writer. What do you do?" Lorna took pity on Sally.

Sally found comfort in Lorna's blue eyes. "I'm Sally Thompson. I'm an attorney."

"Really? That's very interesting. Have you ever been a spy for the CIA?"

"No, but I inadvertently ended up in a CIA training camp in Bosnia."

"Really? How'd that happen?"

Lorna got up and poured the tea as Sally spoke.

"My Grandfather, on my fathers side, helped to build the CIA, or whatever they did back then and my parents worked for the CIA. So my father's mother, you know, Grandma Soucek, raised me and decided after college I should train with the CIA. Except she told me I was doing aid work in Bosnia. Lorna, I was so young and so naïve. I mean I really didn't know, I thought my parents worked as translators."

Sally took a sip of her tea. "I mean who does that? Who puts their only grandchild in a war zone in a CIA camp? What kind of person does that?"

"Someone who feeds off other people's experiences." Lorna nodded.

"That's not," Sally shook her head, "that's just not right. No. And I figured it out too late. It was almost too late." Sally seemed to recede into her thoughts.

Lorna continued with her mock interview. "Really, how'd that happen?"

"Oh, it's a long story but because I have a look about me that says Eastern European, or possibly Eurasian, or even maybe Pacific Islander."

Lorna looked at Sally's wavy dark hair and big brown eyes and nodded. "You could be an Inuit."

"True, but then I wouldn't have been given a gun to defend myself when I was there."

"In Bosnia."

"Yeah, we were in teams of four, then later teams of two. Then one night I was teamed up with another female. Someone from medical or so I thought. Everyone just called her Nurse. Anyway, by this time all pretense as to what we were doing there had been dropped and this Nurse and I had to make a drop. Some scavenger hunt for intel. and we got ambushed by the guy making the drop. It was either him or us." Sally chewed the inside of her mouth. "I shot him."

Lorna watched the disgust crawl across Sally's eyes, down her cheek muscles, across her jowls and form a scowl on her lips.

"Reports were made I'm sure. But my trainer acted like I had ferreted out Kim Philby single handedly. It was disgusting."

"Who's Kim Philby?"

"He's was a British Intelligence officer who became famous after he got caught spying for Russia. Anyway, after I got out of there I made tracks. I declined any CIA job offers. I enrolled in law school and stopped contact with Grandma. I did not hear from my parents again till February 1999, they had a house outside Boston. That's where they staged their death. So I saw a chance to break free. I changed my last name from Soucek to Thompson, and got a job with the housing authority in New York City. I didn't hear from Grandma again till just after 9/11. Then, off and on, we'd exchange Christmas cards."

"But when I was down there, in Phoenix with you. It was like you and Grandma were good buddies or something."

"Yeah. She's good isn't she? Almost had me convinced too. That's what I'm talking about. You can't trust them. They're psychopaths. Whatever they were telling you, it's all just a twisted version of reality."

Lorna looked around. "This is like crazy, you know that right? It's so far from anything – it sounds like you made it up. I know you didn't but, it's just—"

Sally interrupted her and put her hand on Lorna's. "It gets worse."

"Worse than psychopaths in our living room?"

"Then Nurse showed up at my bus stop the night of Tim's murder."

Lorna pulled a face. "The one who was with you when you shot—"

"Yes."

"What the hell?"

"She said she's now with the NSA. And that she's heading up a joint task team that is pulling together units from different agencies and she's overseeing the operation."

"Like the CIA and FBI and NSA all working together? Bah! Bullshit. Everyone knows that's bullshit. They weren't set up to work together. Even *I* know that."

"I know. But I have to play along, especially if we're ever going to find out what happened to Tim."

"What does he have to do with it?"

Sally was careful to keep Tessa's name out of it but said, "Tim worked for Spectorgies and they have a lot of defense contracts with the NSA but they also have technology contracts with other nations."

"Like who?"

"Israel, Poland, Germany, France, and Saudi Arabia I think. But that's not the point. The point is Spectorgies was working on something and apparently Tim got involved. I guess he was informing on them to the NSA and according to Nurse, Time stole a valuable piece of equipment from the contractor and that is what got Tim killed."

Lorna thought for a moment. "Oh Sally, I think she's feeding you a load of crap. I don't believe it. Tim? Was a NSA informant? Come on. Tim's a middle aged surfer dude."

"It's very seductive for people. Plus, they pay their informants. Tax free."

"What does this mean? That you have to play along too? I don't know. I don't think I like this."

"I need to find out what she wants first. Then I'll be able to tell how far into this Tim had gotten."

Lora leaned back in her seat. "It's deceitful." Her mouth puckered as if she just spit out a cherry pit.

"Oh but when you and Tessa are deceitful, what is it, cute?"

Lorna leaned forward and hissed, "No, Sally, it's not. But then again it's not *murder* either."

"I'm sorry. I didn't mean that."

"No, you're right, we live by a double standard. Most southern women do, it's part of our culture. But so is having confidence and good horse sense and putting others before ourselves."

"Do you think I'm lacking in good sense?"

"Well, since we're having a come to Jesus meeting here, sometimes I do. Yes."

Lorna watched Sally's face sag as the words landed on her like a ton of bricks.

"Oh. Did you think this before or after you found out about my parents?"

"Before I found out about your parents I thought it was cute, quirky. Now I don't."

"I did a bad thing, but for what I thought were the right reasons. I see that was a mistake. I hope you can find a way to forgive me. It would be a generous gesture of good will if we could work together in this."

Lorna tilted her head. "A generous gesture of good will? What is this the UN?"

Sally was desperate. "Please don't shave my head."

"What?"

"Tessa told me the lice story. What you did to her."

Lorna gave a deep guttural chuckle.

"It was cruel, Lorna. I don't think I could bare it."

"Why did you tell my sister and father and not me?"

"I didn't. Your sister said she found out through a friend in the CIA."

"My sister has friends in the CIA?"

Sally shrugged. "I guess."

"Is there anything else you've lied about, because now is the time."

"No. Nothing. You know everything else. Everything. Even that *other* thing." Sally added surreptitiously.

"Okay."

"How about you?"

Lorna dropped her shoulders and tilted her head again. "No. Sally. You may have noticed my aversion to metaphorical closets."

"I have."

"So. What do we do now?"

"I'm sure Nurse will get in contact with me. Until then we protect Annie, and yourself from that detective. Maybe get Annie into some grief counseling."

"What about Wallace and Eunice?"

"Who?"

"Your parents."

"Oh. Ignore them. Don't give them any information they can twist up and sell. And if there is any kind of weirdness, you'll have to let me know immediately."

"I just thought about something."

"What?" Sally asked.

"Tessa's cone of silence."

"The frequency jammer? I thought that it gave you a headache."

"It does, but it might come in handy."

"Let's hope it doesn't come to that."

CHAPTER 12

EBB AND FLOW

Lorna watched from her front windows as Roberta took down the tape from across Annie's front door. She retreated from the windows to the kitchen when she saw Roberta turn around and come towards the house. Lorna poured herself a cup of coffee and carried it with her when she heard the knocking at the door.

"Hey." Lorna said. "Come on in."

Roberta opened the screen door and walked in. "I just came by to let you know the detective in charge has released the house. Is Annie still asleep?"

"She is, or possibly in a catatonic state. It's hard to tell."

"Are you serious?"

"Yes. She's not doing well Roberta."

"Oh, I should see her."

"Go right ahead, but if she's asleep, you had better not wake her." Lorna said sternly.

Roberta slipped off her shoes. "Upstairs?"

"Yeah, go ahead."

Lorna went back into the kitchen and listened to Roberta's footfalls upstairs and then heard them come back downstairs.

"Sleeping."

Lorna nodded.

"Has she eaten anything?"

"Mrs. Strangler got her to sip some broth yesterday. I was hoping to get her into the shower today. Maybe a piece of bread."

"What's wrong with her?"

Lorna's eyebrows knitted together and she glared at Roberta. "She sad. Roberta. And probably still in shock. Some people are really not cut out to see murdered people."

"What does that mean?"

"Don't let this job make you callous to human sensitivity, that's all."

"Was I being insensitive by checking in on her? Making sure her house got back open to her?"

"Not if you were doing it for the right reasons."

"Oh, you got it all figured out don't you?" Roberta was on the verge of filling Lorna in on everything she thought Lorna didn't know.

"If I'm incorrect, I'm sure I can rely on you to set me straight."

"You got that right."

"Well?"

"You're taking this too far." Roberta started walking out.

"I'd do the same for you. I wouldn't let you get framed for anything."

Roberta came back to the kitchen door and paused. She had seen Lorna in action on more than a few occasions and Keeling had trusted her implicitly, despite their rancor with one another. "You know, I think you would."

"Yes ma'am."

Roberta nodded. "I'll check back with you later. You guys need some food up in here."

"That's very gracious of you. I think casseroles are the foods for the occasion."

"I'll have my husband stop by, I have a murder to solve."

Lorna nodded. "Thank you Roberta."

Boxes of take out containers and dry goods fill the upstairs office and storage room of the Auld Alliance Café. A large wooden desk sat in the corner with an old style desk lamp and stacks of invoice papers on top. A black rotary phone sat on the edge of the desk atop a stack of three ring binders. Sally wondered how the large leather couch she was sitting on even got into this room in the first place. She was having second thoughts about her parent's appearance on the island and needed to find out more. Eunice finally returned with Wallace and they sat down across from her.

"Let's cut the shit Dad. What is it you guys want? Why are you here?"

"We told you, we've opened this shop. And we want you to give it up."

"Give what up?" Sally played innocent.

"Whatever it is you stole. Sweetheart, you can not imagine the trouble you are in right now." Eunice said.

"I thought you said Annie stole it." Sally blinked.

"Although, I have to say you can really whip up a shit storm!" Wallace laughed. "We never imagined you had it in you."

Eunice added proudly. "Pickles had said, 'either you were complete *enfant terrible* or the best he's ever seen.'"

So they weren't going to answer her lying accusation, she went on. "Who's Pickles?"

"Oh Sweetheart, I always dreamed you would study under him and be his protégée he was the sharpest mind – a complete genius."

"He was an agent?"

"Pfft." Wallace coughed out. "No. Pickles didn't even exist."

"Oh here we go." Sally muttered under her breath. Her mind moved quickly. Was there a way to get them to just tell her what they wanted in a linear fashion? "Okay, who do you think I should turn *it* over to?"

Wallace offered, "Why don't you give it to us and we'll turn it over to the CIA—"

"Or the NSA, Dear. It was, after all, their device to begin with." Eunice spoke over him. "That way we can keep you out of it."

"Who did you say Pickles affiliated with? If he sent you then it should go to them, right? Finders keepers?"

"We didn't—". Wallace started again.

"The FBI?" Eunice answered.

Sally gave a tight smile. "Good. Then the FBI thinks that Tim stole something and I'm supposed to know about it. So, you said before, government contractors were involved. Tim did work for Spectorgies but as a human resource specialist. He went out to different companies working on projects, do you know what other contractor is involved?"

Eunice realized her earlier mistake.

"We don't care." Wallace said. "You're the one who's so high and mighty and now you've gotten yourself in a lot of trouble, we're here to help you. Whether you want to believe that or not, if you're caught with this equipment they can try you for treason. Or worse."

Sally got up from her seat and paced. "You don't know then." She ignored his threats. "Sounds like someone is playing good cop, bad cop. So the FBI has sent you two in as the good cops and someone else is playing bad cop. Who?"

"What do you mean the bad cops?"

"Tim was killed the other night. They slashed his throat. Sound familiar?"

"Sounds Russian." Wallace answered.

"Or the Mossad." Eunice added.

"You think that Russia, or Israel, sent in agents—" Sally rubbed her forehead. "Do you know if your friend, Pickles, sent anyone else?"

"He certainly might have." Eunice answered.

"So the question I'm left with is, did Tim steal some kind of equipment or, as an informant, was he set up to look like he stole it. Wait a second. You said Pickles sent you, but now Pickles is dead. Who are you reporting too?"

"No one. We retired. Pickles simply said that you were in trouble of some kind and we snuck back in and opened the café." Eunice was enjoying this little tete a tete.

"But how? I mean, there are contracts to sign. You have to have credit history."

"Or a lot of cash." Eunice snorted as she laughed.

This was all she was going to get out of these two. Sally searched her mind for the invisible link between the FBI and whoever had killed Tim. As she had originally thought, they were in this thing for their own gain. But they didn't do it or else they wouldn't still be here. If they were reporting to someone, they'd never reveal it, even if they did know who it ultimately turned out to be.

"Look, I appreciate you both coming to warn me. I do. But I hope you can appreciate that I have built a life without you in it. We'll stop in here to see you from time to time but that's it. Don't try to warm up to my partner to get to me either. Don't come around and *pop by* for a visit. If you think you can live with those terms and boundaries then we'll be okay. But if you can't, I'll splash your photos on every website available and I'll raise such a stink you won't be safe in Timbuktu. I hope I've made myself clear." Sally turned and walked out.

Lorna put the phone back in its cradle and sat quietly for a moment. She took a deep breath and slowly released it trying to keep the nausea from escalating. The scream and hysterics from Tim's mother were so palpable Lorna felt her chest tighten in sympathy. That poor woman, first Tim's father dies and now Tim. Not even grandchildren to hang on to. Tim did have a brother, somewhere, Hawaii she thought he had said. That's right, Tim said they didn't get along. Lorna rubbed the tension out of her forehead. Patience jumped into her lap.

"Oh Patience, I need a hug, thank you." Patience sat on her lap letting her squeeze him and offered the top of his head for a kiss. "That was horrible. Seriously, no one should ever have to hear that." Lorna rubbed the back of his ears. "Or say those words."

Images of Tim's body in that pool of blood, Tim laughing, and Tim holding Annie's hand walking down the street flashed into her head like a roulette wheel and landed on Tim's body again. Lorna felt a pang of sadness grip her. What were his last thoughts? Did he even know what had happened? Did he know he was dying?

The devastation of what Annie must be going through, laying upstairs alone in the guestroom, racked her with pain. Lorna clutched Patience close and tears began streaming down her face. The stress of the last week with Tessa, Sally's parents, and Tim was releasing in sobs. She and Annie had been out getting drunk while Tim, a friend and her best friends husband lay dying in his own pool of blood. The nausea she felt moments before had turning in shades of anger, guilt, and pain. She rocked back and forth hugging Patience to her chest as the grief subsided. The moment passed leaving Lorna feeling spent. She lifted her head and released Patience from her arms. When she looked back up, Annie was standing in the doorway. They looked at each other for a moment. Annie looked ten years older, the creases in her face had deepened, she had dark circles beneath her eyes, frown-lines had appeared around her mouth.

Annie opened her mouth and said slowly, "I need help."

Lorna jumped up from her seat and embraced Annie. Annie crumpled in her arms. They stood that way for a few minutes crying and holding each other until Lorna pulled away. "Oh Baby, you need a bath is what you need."

"I'm sorry." Annie said.

"Oh and brush your teeth. Come on." Lorna ushered Annie back upstairs.

Annie sat on the commode as Lorna started the shower and pulled out a fresh toothbrush from it's packaging. "I'll need some fresh clothes."

"I've got some for you."

"Thank you."

Lorna left Annie in the shower and went back downstairs. She looked at her list for the day. She had called Annie's job, and Tim's mom. Bob, end of life arranger, was handling the funeral arrangements in San Jose and putting together a to-do list involving life insurance policies, and notifications for Annie. The divorce wasn't final since they had only signed the papers but had not filed them in any courts, so as far as the law as concerned they were still married. Lorna shook her head. This end of life shit is a lot of work. How are people supposed to handle this while grieving? She put the papers into a file folder and tucked it in between the wall and toaster oven. She heard the shower stop upstairs and poured Annie a cup of coffee when the doorbell rang.

Lorna opened the door to Roberta's son, Daoud, who was proudly holding a tin casserole dish.

"It's from my Mom and Dad, they said they were sorry for your loss." Daoud said.

Lorna poked her head around the corner and saw Tomas sitting in his car. They exchanged waves. "Thank you Daoud, for bringing it to me. That is very gracious and kind of you."

Daoud smiled. Lorna noticed he was missing another tooth. "Your welcome." He said and handed the dish over to Lorna. Then he ran and leapt down her front stairs. Lorna turned and gave his father, Tomas, another wave before shutting the door.

She put the casserole dish in the refrigerator, grabbed the coffee cups, and headed back upstairs.

Annie opened the door to the bathroom and looked across the hall at Lorna sitting on the now made up guest bed. "You know, I think you have more water pressure than we do." Annie said as she hung her towel up on the rack.

"Well, I think this house was remodeled after yours." Lorna cast a glance around the room. Why is Annie talking about the water pressure?

Annie came in and sat on the other side of the bed. "I'll never be able to repay Mrs. Strangler for the kindness she's shown me."

"Oh she's just trying to build up her poker night clientele." Lorna laughed.

"I think those little pills she's been feeding me have finally kicked in."

"Mrs. Strangler is drugging you?"

"I thought you knew."

"What is she giving you?"

"How should I know?"

Lorna turned and looked searchingly at Annie for a moment. "Well, how do you feel?"

"Kinda numb, and thirsty. It comes out of a prescription bottle." Annie explained.

Lorna shook her head. "Well, okay, I guess, I mean you're out of bed and talking."

Lorna was able to explain to Annie where things stood as of right now. She explained about Bob, the end of life guy, the detective, Chris, Roberta, and Sally's parents, what her boss had said, and finally her phone call to Tim's mother.

"How long have I been out?" Annie asked.

"Just a day, today is Thursday." Lorna answered.

"I think I'd like to go back to bed now."

"You have to go give Chris your statement. I'm just waiting for Sally to get back home and we'll take you."

"Bert and Ernie?"

"Sally's made a small palace for them in the garage complete with a heater. They're okay for now. Angela is taking them to the park twice a day."

"Twice? Wow, I only go once with them. Sometimes I skip a day." Annie said regretfully.

Lorna gripped Annie's arm. "One thing at a time. One little step, then another little step."

A dark cloud passed over Annie's face. "They say God doesn't give you more than you can handle."

Lorna grinned mischievously. "Horse shit. Then why are there insane asylums?"

Annie searched Lorna's face until Lorna couldn't take it anymore and cracked a grin.

Annie finally smiled back. "You're awful sometimes, you know that?"

"Yes I am!" Lorna announced, getting up from the bed. "Come on, lets go try that casserole Tomas brought."

Annie stayed where she was and looked down. "You're doing that thing. I can't this time Lorna. I can't go that fast. Little steps."

Lorna sat back down. "Annie. I understand the pull of grief. It can be comforting. Like, if I can hang on to my grief, I can hang on to that person I lost. I get that, in Technicolor. And I don't want to push you, but believe me, there *will* be time to grieve and be lonely and sad. Only we have to get you through this investigation. And you cannot hide in here and let the days pass like an empty parade. The next four seasons of your life are going to pass, whether you are in them or not."

"You're good at that."

"Grieving?"

"No, that 'buck up' thing you do."

"I am, aren't I? I could be a motivational speaker. But then I'd have to deal with people. And there ain't enough money in the *world.*" Lorna got back up from the bed, "Come on Scarlet O'Hara. Food. Attorney. Drugs with Mrs. Strangler."

Roberta watched from her unmarked police cruiser as the car carrying Annie, Sally, and Lorna pulled up to the stop sign and turned left. She waited another moment or two before getting out of her own car and walking up to Mrs. Strangler's house. The door opened before she knocked. "You ready?" Mrs. Strangler asked.

"Yeah." As Roberta looked down at the tiny old woman she wished she had a camera. Mrs. Strangler was wearing a black running outfit and a black sock cap. She wore her black purse on the crook of her elbow and slipped her keys into the side pocket after she locked her front door. Roberta smiled. "You look like you're going on a madcap caper."

The irony was not lost on the ever-fashionable Mrs. Strangler. At eighty-*seven* she still had a sharp mind. "Well I can't wear couture, not for this, I have to be able to move." She moved her arms back and forth boxing air as she made her small shuffling steps out into the street.

Roberta let them into the back gate of Annie's house. Mrs. Strangler used her spare key, unlocking the glass patio door.

"What the hell happened here?" Mrs. Strangler demanded walking inside.

"I was hoping you could tell me."

Mrs. Strangler picked up a broken porcelain figurine off the floor. "Oh what a shame, look at this." She carefully placed part of the figurine back on the shelf.

Roberta looked around the kitchen, a few of the drawers and cupboard doors were open and she didn't remember that from the night they found Tim.

She heard Mrs. Strangler gasp and rushed into the living room. Mrs. Strangler was cupping her hand over her mouth and glaring down at the dried bloodstain on the floor. Flies had found their way to the room and Roberta careful escorted Mrs. Strangler back to the kitchen to sit down.

Mrs. Strangler turned on her. "Roberta Fitzgerald. How could you? How could you ever suspect Annie could do such a thing? What's wrong with this picture? I'll tell you, Annie Doughall could no more cause this than I could."

Roberta squatted down in an effort to connect with Mrs. Strangler. "I don't think that. I don't. That's why I brought you here. But look, I know that Annie couldn't have done this, and you know that. But the man in charge of this investigation is looking to use Annie as a notch on his belt. If I don't come up with something, anything that proves her innocence then that man is going to drag her through the courts. And it won't cost him a dime, but it *will* destroy her, financially and emotionally. So please help me here. Look around, you know Annie's jewelry, her valuables - if this was a robbery then something's got to be missing."

Mrs. Strangler nodded. "I'll go upstairs. She probably keeps her jewelry there."

"Thank you." Roberta stood up and went upstairs into Annie's office. "What the hell am I looking for?" She mumbled to herself.

The whole 'giving a statement ordeal' didn't turn out as bad as Lorna had anticipated. She was prepared to sedate Annie and to carry her out of the attorney's office. But whatever Mrs. Strangler had doped Annie with was working. She only had a few breakdowns, which could have been expected. She also had expected Chris, the attorney, to handle Annie with kit gloves. But he didn't. He simply kept everything factual. As a matter of fact, more emotion is poured out when someone reports a stolen bicycle than what Chris employed here. But he seemed to understand that Annie's grief was ebbing and flowing like a tide. Lorna leaned back in her chair and watched, she could learn a few things from this guy.

As they left through the parking garage Lorna offered, "Well Annie, now that we're in the city maybe you'd like to eat somewhere special. Like one of your vegetarian places, where they serve dirt."

Annie clucked her tongue. "I was thinking we could go back to the island, like maybe *Auld Alliance*."

"OH!" Sally bellowed, stopping in her tracks.

"OH! Touché!" Lorna smiled.

They climbed back into the car and Sally turned around. "You know what I'd like? Some cupcakes."

"Oh yeah, let's pick some up on our way out." Lorna agreed and turned around to face the back seat. "Annie, do you mind?"

Annie turned her head out of the window. "I don't care. That's fine." The tide was turning again, Lorna noticed.

Sally carefully steered the car around the parking garage when Annie spoke up. "Do you know what's weird?"

"Besides the fact that Lorna and Tessa used to play a game called *Helen Keller*?" Sally offered.

"Hey, I learned brail and ASL playing Helen Keller." Lorna took mock offense.

"Please, I'm serious. Not one person has asked me if I might know of someone who'd want Tim dead. Nobody has even asked me what I think may have happened, in my own home." Annie broke down again hiding her face in her hands and choked out, "They all think I did it."

"Pull over." Lorna directed.

"I'm *pulling* over." Sally snapped back.

Lorna took her seatbelt off and climbed into the backseat with Annie. "Okay. First of all." Sally and Lorna exchanged a glance in the review mirror. "First of all, no one but that Fat Head detective thinks you had *anything* to do with it. And Annie, you have *teams* of people trying to work on this, to protect you, find the killer, and try to get you through this. Roberta is seriously breaking with protocol to go around that Fat Head's back and find at least one clue. The reason no one has been bothering you is because Sally and I have forbid it. So if you're mad, then be mad at us. And that's fine but do you really want to deal with all that shit now?"

Annie shook her head and bawled out, "I just don't understand."

Sally reached back and put her hand on Annie's knee. "Sssh."

Lorna let Annie cry for another minute before saying, "You know what I think?"

Annie shook her head.

"I think we should get back to the island and get some of those pills from Mrs. Strangler."

"What?" Sally asked.

"Mrs. Strangler has been getting Annie high."

Annie laughed at the image and leaned back over. "Aah, shit. You may be right."

Sally was aghast. "Are you serious?"

"No, but she's been slipping Annie *something*."

Annie nodded and blew her nose. "I thought it was medicine, from the hospital."

Sally turned forward and started laughing and accidentally blew the car horn.

Lorna broke up the laughter. "It's not really funny, she could be poisoning Annie with something or getting her addicted to some old expired drug that's decomposing into heroin."

They all broke out in laughter again. Finally, Sally started to pull out in traffic again.

"Sally, one night you brought home some lasagna, like we had to cook it, but it was all pre-made."

"Yeah. It's from a place near my office."

"Can we stop there, is it near the cupcake place?"

"Yeah, it's on the way. As a matter of fact, we can just park the car, you guys go get the cupcakes and I'll go get the lasagna."

"Annie, is that okay?"

"Of course. Thank you."

San Francisco is the only city in the entire country where can you find a place like Eat Me. The front of the store has refrigerators pushed up against the walls and a mini two-sided grocery shelf in the middle. The shelves and refrigerator units are filled daily with fresh home made foods, pasta's, bread's, sausages, salads, lasagna's, meatloaf, etc. Everyday, by lunchtime the food that was cooked in the morning and shelved or refrigerated is completely gone. So in the afternoon they replenish the shelves with more food and by six o'clock, when they close, those shelves are completely empty again. Sally regularly bought food for lunch at Eat Me.

But she would never bring Lorna here. Next to the cashiers stand were two small café tables, and a small sink station that also held a microwave and a small toaster oven. Almost everyday, the two-café tables are occupied by some of the city's large population of mentally ill and drug addicted homeless people.

One afternoon in particular Sally saw a young boy sitting at the café table eating. Sally handed the cashier a twenty-dollar bill and said, "Whatever he wants."

The cashier handed Sally back her money. "You're the fourth person."

But today there was no sad 'homeless mother trying to feed her children' scenario's. Today a homeless man stood at the sink giving himself a sponge bath. The smell gagged Sally and she had to turn her head away. Which is why Sally would never bring Lorna to The Eatery. She tried desperately to keep her watering eyes forward to the cashier. The cashier smiled wide at Sally as if there wasn't a man standing two feet away from her washing his crusty armpits.

After Sally made her transaction, she turned to leave and saw Nurse standing at the doorway waiting for her.

"You're not going to eat that are you?"

"What do you want?"

"Just a quick conversation."

"The device that was stolen was software housed device for cloaking satellites. They call it the Aurora."

"I don't know what the means."

"Basically it traps light rays and—"

"Hey." Sally stopped walking. "I *don't* want to have this conversation with you." But it was exactly the missing information Sally needed.

"You have to find that box, it's going to be silver or black, smaller than a shoebox but larger than a cell phone." Nurse grabbed Sally's arm, causing Sally to drop the lasagna tray. Nurse reached down to help Sally pick it up but Sally pushed her away.

Nurse grabbed Sally's arm and the tray again as Sally started walking away.

"Just stop a minute." Nurse ordered her. "I would not be here if there was another way. I'm trying to help you and help his wife. Now look, we know he took it. An FBI agent already corroborated the story and that person is facing treason. We've got informants and every branch of the services looking for this thing. Now damn it, it had better not turn up under my section. There are only a couple of places that thing can be, you just make sure it's not in that house or on that island."

Sally glared at Nurse. "You done threatening me? His wife doesn't know anything. If Tim stole that device, *if he stole it*, she doesn't know a damn thing about it. But. I'm going to look for it for you. I'll turn that house upside down, *for you*. If I don't find it, you have got to go away. I don't want to see you, hear from you, or even sense you might be in a mile of me or my partner."

"That's all I'm asking."

"Fine." Sally turned abruptly and continued walking down the street. Nurse had just confirmed for her what she had suspected from what her parents told her. It was time to have a conversation with Annie.

The Rot is Deep

CHAPTER 13

TRUTH WILL OUT

"That was excellent." Lorna wiped her mouth with her napkin.

"You keep feeding me like this, I might move in." Mrs. Strangler smiled.

"And we have cupcakes for dessert." Annie added flatly.

"Oh no, not for me. I have to watch my sugar." Mrs. Strangler waved it off as Sally rose and collected everyone's plates.

"Well, I have something to talk about." Mrs. Strangler announced.

"Coffee or tea, anyone?" Sally asked.

"Yes please." Lorna piped up.

"Decaf?" Mrs. Strangler asked.

"The tea is caffeine free, is that okay?" Sally answered.

Lorna got up and cleared the rest of the dishes in one swoop. "I'll bring it in to the living room, you guys go ahead."

"I can help." Annie got up with her.

"No, I know what this is about." Lorna nodded to Mrs. Strangler. "You and Sally go ahead."

"She's right." Sally added, "We'll just be in her way." She continued ahead to the living room.

Annie froze and whispered to Lorna, "What is it?"

"She's just going to give you an update from Roberta. It's okay, no bad news."

Annie reluctantly followed Mrs. Strangler and Sally to the living room.

Lorna quickly rinsed the dishes and loaded them into the dishwasher. As she finished wiping the kitchen table she heard a light tapping on the kitchen door. She glanced over to the door and the tapping came again.

Lorna opened the door to a food deliveryman who held up a steaming bag of Chinese food. "We didn't order any take out."

"65 Saint Charles Place." The young man had dropped the 'el' sound in the word 'place' and had replaced it with an 'ahr' sound.

The man's folly was lost on Lorna. "No. I'm sorry."

He shoved the bag at Lorna and said without any trace of a dialect. "Take it, there's information inside. I'll be in touch."

Lorna looked bewildered.

"Tim good man, we give extra sauce." He said with exaggerated head nods and backed away from the door.

Lorna grabbed the bag, shut and bolted the door, whipped around and opened the cabinet under the sink dumping the food bag in the trashcan just in time. Sally and Annie stood at the kitchen door as Lorna slammed the cabinet, whirled back around, and righted herself.

"Who was that?" Sally asked.

"Who?" Lorna gave a mocking grin and snorted. "Or what? When was the last time we took the trash out? Holy Moses. When did we eat fish?"

"I thought I heard you talking to someone." Sally said accusingly.

"Yeah, I was gasping for breath! You get the tea, I'm taking this mess out." Lorna opened the cabinet. "Stand back!"

"I'll do it, Lorna." Annie said. "I want to check on the dogs anyway."

"No. It is not for the faint of heart. And you're our guest, Sally can you get the tea for me and take it in—"

Lorna didn't finish her sentence. She grabbed the entire trashcan and left.

She didn't put the trashcan down until she got to the street bin and there she started rooting through the bag of Chinese food. Seeing nothing at first she opened a carton and saw a plastic bag containing a small notebook enmeshed in a gooey, chunky liquid. Carefully opening the baggie she delicately pulled out the notebook and tossed the remaining trash from the can into the bin, forgetting to close the garbage bag beforehand. She stuffed the notebook under her back pants waistband and headed back inside.

Mrs. Strangler finished her tea and placed the cup on a cork drink holder. Lorna smiled at Mrs. Strangler and nodded. "I think that's the best plan I've heard in a long while."

"But I don't think, I mean, how would I know if anything was stolen? I haven't been back to the house." Annie asked.

"He doesn't know that." Sally said holding her palms up.

"Roberta says it will throw enough of a shadow over his investigation he will be forced to look into it and if he doesn't you'll at least show that he suppressed evidence." Mrs. Strangler explained.

"But is he? Suppressing evidence?" Annie asked

"We don't know. That's the problem." Sally said.

"So I walk in, and tell them I'd like to report a robbery. How do you know they won't recognize my name and put me with that Fat Head detective?"

"Because Roberta is going to call us when he goes to lunch. By the way his name is Fathid. I may have mislead you with calling him Fat Head." Lorna said.

The phone rang and Sally jumped up to get it.

Lorna continued. "Roberta is going to be there when you arrive and take you to the, what is it, robbery division? Whatever, she's going to take you to the person you need to talk to."

Sally picked up the phone and was surprised to hear Katie's voice on the line.

"I'm sorry to bother you so late, but I just got home and wanted to give you a heads up." Katie said urgently.

"Oh, no." Sally corrected herself, "I mean, it's fine, what happened?"

"Today, two men came in and went straight into Scott's office. They were there for a few minutes and then they all went back down the hall. So I gave them a minute and followed them. They were in your office and Scott was at your computer terminal and the two guys were going through your office, like they were looking for something."

"What?"

"I don't know, but then I walked back a few minutes later and they were holding up files and looking through them."

Sally thought this for a minute. She kept all her personal papers at home, what could they hope to find?

"Sally?"

"Yeah, I was just trying to think about my case load. I don't think I have anything pressing or hot right now."

"Well listen, then Scott walked them to the door and I kinda raise my eyebrows at him when he comes back by my desk and he mouths FBI at me and shrugs."

"What?"

"I know."

"Oh shit, Katie, you know I did bring some work home. But wait, anything I have you can also find on the lexicon or the database. I just brought that stuff home in paper form so I can look over it. Was it just my office?"

"Yeah."

"That's weird."

"I know." Katie agreed.

"Well, I have to stop in tomorrow anyway. I'll swing by Scott's office and see if he says anything to me. They may have just been looking for my notes on a case or something."

"Sure."

"Gosh, you really do have my back. Thanks Katie. Anything else?"

"Same day, different shit."

"Right, I'll see you tomorrow. Thanks again."

Sally hung the phone up and rubbed a hand across her mouth. She felt the buzzards circling and forced herself not to panic. It was probably nothing, just bad timing.

She walked back into the living room and sat down before she noticed everyone looking at her. "Oh. My office, I have to go in tomorrow and clear a couple of things up. I need to get a couple of cases to my boss."

"When?" Lorna wanted to know.

"I'll do it in the afternoon, after lunch."

"I'm going to call Angela now." Lorna got up and walked back into the kitchen.

Mrs. Strangler explained to Sally, "Lorna's going to see if Angela can meet her at Annie's and help clean up the place a bit before Annie has to go back over there with the police."

Sally nodded. "That's a great Annie. So in the morning you can take your dogs out, which should be relaxing, right? And then deal with Bob and they'll do the tidying up, that way if you have to go back in the afternoon—"

"I'd like to say something here." Mrs. Strangler interjected. "I have an extra bedroom too."

Sally looked over to Annie who sat placidly. Without a shadow of a doubt, at some point this evening the Queen of England had slipped Annie a dose of whatever concoction she pulled from her medicine chest. "That's fine, but remember, we need Annie sober for at least until after " she wanted to say the funeral but thought better of it, "Sunday."

Tears welled up in Annie's eyes and she shook her head.

"I'm just saying, Annie should know she has more than one place to lay her head." Mrs. Strangler began before catching the wink and grin Sally gave her. Mrs. Strangler nodded in agreement. "I believe there were some cupcakes promised this evening."

Lorna shut the door to their bedroom as Sally crawled into bed. Lorna pulled out a notebook from the back of her pants and flopped it on the bed next to her.

"What is it?"

"Remember the stinky garbage incident earlier?"

"Yes."

"Actually, you did hear voices. This guy, a Chinese deliver guy, showed up and gave this to me." Lorna pointed at the notebook. "And he said there is information in there, and that he'd be in touch."

"What did he look like?"

"He was Asian, like 5'8-ish, around my height."

"And he just handed this to you?"

"No, it was packed in the food, in a zip-lock baggie."

"Now, what happened?"

"Dude, this isn't difficult. An Asian man came to the kitchen door and tried to deliver a bag of Chinese food. I said 'no, we didn't order'. He said, 'take it there's information inside' then 'I'll be in touch'."

Sally pulled a face, "You didn't think to mention this earlier?"

"How could I?" Lorna realized she was speaking too loud and moved close to Sally on the bed and hissed, "Oh and by the way *Annie*, while you're *lying* to the police and planning your husbands funeral, we think we know *why* he was killed but not *who* did it."

"Okay, I'm sorry." Sally picked the notebook up and flipped through it. "What is it with you sticking stuff down your pants anyway?" She frowned at it and put it back down.

"It's gibberish."

"It's in code."

"Nothing's easy is it?"

"Nope. You wanna bet Annie will be the only person who can read it?"

"Well, you're good at puzzles and stuff, why don't you give it a whirl?"

"Because I'm exhausted."

"You're the secret agent. Didn't you get trained in ciphers?"

"No. I didn't."

"Did you stop by your parents today?"

"Please, don't call them that."

"Um." Lorna knitted her brow and said slowly, "Then what would you like to call them?"

"Whatever. Listen these are the people your sister is always warning you about."

"Okay. Did the Whatever's say anything more about that assassin thing?"

"No, Lorna, they just talk out there ass and hope something sticks to you."

"Ew. Then I'll look at it tomorrow, if it's personal, I'll give it to Annie *after* she comes back from the police station. After all that's over with, one thing at a time. It's not that I want to withhold evidence, mind you. But I'm afraid he'll turn it around on us. Should we tell Roberta? No, I don't know. Am I being a control freak?"

"Probably. I think you're very tired though. But the fact that you just admitted it is a good sign. Speaking of control freaks, have you spoken to your sister?"

"Not today. I'll call her tomorrow."

Sally thought about the phone call from Katie. "It's probably nothing. Seriously, nothing, but you know the phone call I got tonight?"

"Yeah."

"It was Katie from work. She said that the FBI tossed my office."

"What?"

"Yeah. Which I think means they are heading here tomorrow."

"Don't they need a warrant or something?"

"I'm sure they had it."

"Well, what do we do?"

"Cooperate."

"What do we do with this?" Lorna held up the notebook.

"Take it back over to Annie's house." Sally picked up the notebook and sighed. "What is that one food the nutritionist told you to stay clear of?"

"Br—"

Suddenly Sally made several fake sign language movements with her hand and put her finger up to her mouth in a hush.

"Bread." Sally cut her off and then slowly tapped her own ears. "From here on out, we need to be more careful of what we *eat*. We need to keep our *health* up for Annie."

Lorna nodded, she knew exactly what Sally was trying to tell her with the fake sign language. She took the notebook and held it out like a sandwich and mimicked taking a bite of it. Then raised her eyebrows questioningly.

"Yes." Sally nodded and pointed her finger down indicating downstairs.

"I'll take it in the morning then." Lorna confirmed.

"I can do it." Sally offered.

"This is getting stupid."

"Yes. And what's worse is I think we're just at the beginning." Sally stretched out in the bed. "Are you still mad at me?"

"No."

"Do you love me still?"

"Yes, but I'm still disappointed and a little sad you didn't trust me."

"I am too. It was foolish of me. And what's even worse is I was the only person who could have prevented that. Ya' know?"

"Well. You tried to control something that wasn't in your control." Lorna leaned in close to Sally and whispered, "Which is what I'm a little worried about right now."

"Listen, I think you're doing the right things here. I trust your judgment, entirely. Your sister once told me you had reptilian instincts."

"Oh well, fuck her."

"I think it was a compliment."

At nine a.m. Angela knocked on Annie's front door and Lorna answered. "Angela, thank you so much for coming." Two more ladies popped out from behind Angela. "Oh." Lorna wasn't expecting these other women to show up and didn't quite know what to say.

"This is Nouri and Maria. I told them about what happened and they want to help."

"Oh that's wonderful. I'll just have to run to the ATM though. I didn't plan on any more people—" Lorna did not want to scare these ladies off by any means. That morning they had decided it would be better if Sally stayed with Annie as she made the funeral plans. And then Sally could go to work in the afternoon while Mrs. Strangler went to San Jose with Annie.

Angela turned to the woman and said something quickly in Spanish that Lorna couldn't quite catch. Both women shook their heads no. Angela turned back to Lorna, "No, they do not want you to do that."

Lorna sighed and looked at these two women. Either they were going to case the place to rob later or they were just 'good people', as her father would say. Lorna nodded at the women. "Muchas gracias," and moved back for the women to enter.

The two women gasped when they saw the flies multiplying in Tim's dried blood spread out like a grotesque floor mat. They both crossed themselves.

Lorna looked at the stain and back at the women. "Comencemos arriba?"

The women nodded and they all headed upstairs.

Sally winked at Katie as she walked in. Katie gave a quick covert glance around the office before nodding acknowledgment back. Sally purposely took the long route so she could pass by her boss's office before she nonchalantly settled herself back into her own office. A moment later Scott showed up and shut the door behind him.

"Oh hi." Sally said continuing to shuffle through her papers but stopped at the appropriate moment. "I just wanted to bring this stuff back in before Monday. I finished a couple of cases, so I shouldn't fall too far behind."

"Okay."

Sally looked up at him. "What's up?"

He sat down across from her. "I don't know. Why would the FBI want to go through your desk and papers?"

Sally's mouth fell open. "What? What were they looking for?"

"They said it was a routine inspection."

Sally glanced around her office. "For what? Is it a new routine?"

He leaned across her desk. "Come on. The FBI *does not* just show up to do an inspection of a federal housing staff attorney. Look, I'll help you as best I can, but you have to tell me what's going on."

Sally paused long enough to simulate she was thinking of an answer. She looked at her computer screen and then at the papers on her desk and back up to Scott.

"The only thing I can think of is Tim's murder. I mean this guy investigating it, the detective, is seriously a fat head. He has no idea what he's doing, I think. And ya' know, Tim worked for Spectorgies."

"The defense contractors?"

Sally nodded. "Mm hmm."

"Doing what?"

"He was a human resource specialist."

"Good God, Sally, stay out of that."

"I know. We're just trying to get his wife through it. She's just devastated and that detective is hell bent on prosecuting her."

Scott nodded. "Just because you're paranoid, don't mean they're not after you."

Sally nodded along with him and said knowingly, "I'll bet it has something to do with that. I mean other than that, let them look." She lifted up some papers and dropped them. "I'm an open book here."

"No, I know that. That's why I was so shocked."

"I appreciate the help, but seriously, there's nothing here. Let them look and if they need to reach me I'll be at home. Except Sunday, I'll be in San Jose for the funeral."

"Well thanks, that makes me feel better." Scott chuckled. "And look if you need more time helping her through this, just call. We'll shift some of the case load around, okay?"

"Thanks Scott."

By the time the boxes in the dining room were carefully refilled and stacked neatly in Annie's dining room it was already noon. The three women had worked non-stop for three hours cleaning the upstairs, the back part of the downstairs, and repacking up Tim's personal belongings in the dining room.

They were standing in the large doorway between the kitchen and the living room.

"Ay dios mio." Maria said staring at the large stain.

Nouri crossed herself again.

Lorna turned and smiled to them. "I think you guys have done enough for today. I simply can't ask you to tackle this. Let me handle the kitchen and this." Lorna indicated the stain.

Angela turned to the two women and quickly translated for her. Maria then said something so fast Lorna could not follow along.

"Oh Maria, slow down. Please." Lorna pleaded.

Angela held a hand up to stop Lorna talking and the three women rapidly conversed.

Angela turned to Lorna. "You have to have professional cleaners come in to clean this. They have special chemicals. Maria thinks you should wear gloves and get the worst of it up so you don't have to worry about the flies but then throw a rug on it - until the cleaners come."

Lorna nodded. She had put the money she was to pay Angela and the money for lunch in her pocket. She pulled it out now and handed it to Angela. "Please take this. There's some extra for lunch for you guys, if you want. Thank you so much. Muchas Gracias." Lorna nodded to the women.

"Thank you, I'm going to get the dogs now. Are you sure you don't need anything else?"

"No. Angela. You have done so very much for Annie. But I'm going to guess that she'll want to keep you on for the dog walking for a while. Is that okay?"

"Yes, of course. But what are you going to do for your lunch?"

"You know I think it's better I handle this." Lorna nodded at the stain. "Before I eat."

"Oh yes. Okay. Maybe I come check on you after I take the dogs out." Angela said leading the women out of the house.

Lorna left the front door open as the women made their way down the sidewalk. What the hell, some people really are just *good people*, she thought. She felt a bit of shame for thinking otherwise about these complete strangers who showed up just to help the friend of a client.

Lorna had used Annie's towels as a sponge reef around the worst of the bloodstain to help absorb the warm water and vinegar she had poured over it. As it soaked she scrubbed down the stray streaks off the coffee table and wall. Annie would probably have to buy new towels but she couldn't think of any other way to clean this up in the short amount of time she had left.

She wondered what could be keeping Sally so long but continued working, sopping up the worst of what had become a thick, dark goo and used a scrub brush over it. She let her mind float from thought to thought as she worked. There had to be a certain amount of planning on Tim's part in this. Had he waited to show up when he knew Annie was out for the evening? And now she knew there was an accomplice that Chinese Delivery guy knew something. Even if Tim had just said, 'in case of my death, deliver this notebook to Annie.' Then that was at least something to go on. She remembered the cellar door again and stopped scrubbing. No, she just can't go down there, that cellar is so creepy. She'll get Sally or Roberta to go check it out.

Deep down, she did trust Sally. If you think about it, she thought to herself, she and her dad and Tessa are all Sally really have - obviously, she doesn't trust her own parents, and for good reason. Sally screwed up, and it was kinda self-fish but at least it was a noble reason for the selfishness. Or she told herself it was. People really are nuts. This whole thing is nuts and she should try to stay out of it and keep Annie and Sally out of it.

But really, Annie is going to do what she's going to do. She'd like to keep her friend safe. At least out of jail for something she didn't do but beyond that, with Sally's background, it would be better if they let Annie in on what is really happening. Then let her guide her own life. She splashed the bucket of water and bleach mixture down on the floor. The mixture would probably ruin the wood, she thought. But perhaps it can be sanded down and re-stained or they can just replace the affected wood slats.

After the funeral, next Monday, she will sit Annie down, give her the notebook and fill Annie in on the whole thing. Lorna rubbed her eyes while the bucket filled with fresh water. Maybe there is something in the notebook about a funeral. What if Tim wanted to be cremated? She needed to decode it tonight, it can't be that hard, she thought.

"Okay last step." Lorna said aloud. As she mopped the remainder of the liquid's up. There was nothing else to be done. But the stain on the wood was still there. They'll have to put a rug over it before Annie gets here and then have the slats replaced.

"Hello?"

Lorna jumped back and gasped. The voice came from the screen door. "Oh shit. You scared me."

"I'm sorry."

Lorna put the mop down on the floor and walked over to the screen door. "It's okay, I was just lost in my thoughts."

"Are you Annie?"

"No, I'm a neighbor, but can I help you with something?"

"Well, I was supposed to meet Tim."

"Oh."

"My name is Bob. Bob Pardee."

"I'm Lorna. Um." Lorna paused.

"I was supposed to meet Tim and get some work files from him."

"Do you work with Tim?"

"No, not directly. I'm an associate."

"Oh geez. You obviously haven't heard. Tim was murdered the other day."

"What!"

"I'm so sorry." Lorna opened the screen door. "Why don't you come in?"

Through the screen Lorna hadn't noticed the man was wearing a toupee. It was a good one but even still, it fascinated her and she struggled to make eye contact with him and not reach over and pet the toupee.

"What happened?" He asked sincerely and then saw the bucket and stain Lorna had been working on. "Oh my God. What happened?"

"We think it was an intruder, like a robbery gone wrong. That's all they know."

He walked around the stain and did what Lorna thought was an odd cursory glance around the house. It was an odd gesture for someone who just had a shock, Lorna thought. He settled down again and pulled his glasses off his face and put a hand on his hip. "This is awful. Did they take anything?"

"I don't know about that. I'm just trying to help Annie out, she's devastated."

"I thought they were divorcing? Tim said they had been fighting."

"I guess, but it wasn't finalized." Lorna watched him with growing concern as he became animated again, putting his glasses back on his face and looking around.

"Well now I don't know what to do. Do you happen to know where those files are?"

Lorna suddenly felt all of her senses go into overdrive. Sally had told her they would have to be careful. She needed to get this guy out of here and she struggled to keep her voice light. "No, but are you the guy from St. Louis? 'Cause Tim had said he was there, like a while back. Maybe—"

"Yes."

Lorna picked up a large book from the coffee table and flipped through the pages. "Because Tim has never been to St. Louis. I know *that* for a fact. Who are you?"

The man jammed his hands into his coat pockets again and seemed to stand straight up, adding three inches to his height. "Whatever man, look, I was just sent here to get Tim's work stuff. Okay? I didn't even know the guy."

He's got to be a cop, she thought. Rising up to her full height as well, she folded her arms around the book, pressing it tightly to her chest and said, "No, you look, Bob, you tell whoever sent you nothing is leaving this house without a court order."

Bob nonchalantly glanced around the room shaking his head.

Lorna took a menacing step forward. "Yeah, tell your boss—"

Lorna did not hear the thudding silencer shots from Bob Pardee's coat pocket, she only felt intense heat and pressure like giant hot bee stings rip into her chest and collapsed on the floor in the remains of Tim's blood.

"Fine. I'll get them myself." Bob Pardee said and stepped over Lorna as he went back into the dining room to finish the job he started.

Also by M. Saylor Billings

The O Line Mysteries

Book 1: *Saint Charles Place*
Book 2: *The Disaster Relief Club*
Book 3: *The Rot is Deep*
Book 4: *Red, White, and Scotch*

Writing as Lorna Tollison

Nobody, really, likes you.
A guide to insouciance.

Nobody, really, reads you.
A guide to self-publishing

ABOUT THE AUTHOR

Saylor Billings lives with her family in Northern California. She is a writer and producer for Billibatt Productions.